TRINITY ACADEMY

F🜃LCON

Cover Designer: Sybil Wilson, PopKitty Design

Cover Model: Andrew Biernat

Photographer Credit: Wander Book Club Photography

TABLE OF CONTENTS

Dedication

Leeann.

A twenty-hour power outage and hundreds of kilometers didn't stop us from getting together, so we could create the Trinity Series.

Thank you for listening to endless hours of voice clips and for talking me off the edge with every release.

Songlist

Synopsis

Wealth and power make them untouchable.
The monarchs of Trinity Academy.

Falcon Reyes.
With a sharp, intelligent look, he reeks of arrogance
wrapped in an icy layer of indifference.
A life of luxury has left him with the notion that everything
is attainable.
Power. Wealth. Status.

He's a god, and I a mere mortal.
He's Jupiter, and I am Mercury.
There's so much power in this man.
He has the kind of influence most people can't even begin
to imagine.

And me... I'm an eighteen-year-old girl who managed to
make him lose control.
I'm the girl who showed him there's a kaleidoscope of
colors outside the high walls of his black and white world.

Prologue

Falcon

Sitting at Club 55 while overlooking Pamplona beach on our vacation in Spain, aggravation fills me as I watch Grayson and his posse of friends head in our direction.

Grayson fucking Stateman. With his sharp features and furtive eyes, one look at him is enough to ruin my day. West and Serena being here with him only add to my annoyance.

"I'm getting tired of this bullshit," I murmur, but it's loud enough for Mason and Lake to hear. The three of us have been best friends since birth, where Grayson has been our nemesis. Our families are at constant war with the Statemans in the business world.

Lazily turning their heads, Mason and Lake glance in the direction I'm scowling.

"Fuck, how does Serena always know where we're at?" Mason asks, a pissed off look darkening his features.

"She probably heard it from our mothers," Lake says, and resting his head back, he closes his eyes. "Mason, don't get into a fight with West."

I swear Lake can sleep anywhere. He's the chilled one in our group, whereas Mason is the fighter.

Mason clenches his jaw, growling, "If he starts a fight, I'll be sure to finish it." It won't take much for Mason and West to tear into each other, and it's the last thing I'm in the mood for during our summer vacation.

Where Grayson and I are locked in a constant battle for the top spot of our social circle, Mason and West hate each other with a consuming vengeance. It's been that way since the car accident Mason's sister died in.

"Gentlemen," Serena smiles, her green eyes sharp and vindictive. Her styled ginger hair hangs in perfect waves over her shoulders. Dressed in the latest fashion from *Versace*, she looks elegant as always. Having known her for years, I see through the mask of sophistication which hides a viper you don't want to get into bed with.

"I'd call you a lady, but we both know I'd be lying," Mason sneers, the energy coming off him patronizing and explosive.

"Mason… charming as always." Filled with annoyance, Serena's gaze sweeps over the table to where I'm sitting.

An alluring smile forms around her lips as her eyes meet mine. "Falcon, what a lovely surprise bumping into you here of all places."

Lake lets out a soft chuckle, then lazily mutters, "Surprise my ass. Montecito's socialites spread news faster than a wildfire."

Her eyes snap to Lake, but picking her battles wisely, she lets his comment go and focuses her attention back on me. Everyone knows attacking Lake in any way is off-limits. It's a line no one is willing to cross, knowing it will bring out the worst in Mason and I. Lake is the kindest soul with a heart of gold, which makes Mason and I overly protective of him.

"Mother says they're in talks with your family about a merger," Serena says, her voice filled with premature triumph.

I grind my teeth and shooting Serena a steely glare, I reply, "Merger? You call an arranged marriage between us a merger?"

"Of course. Combining our assets will make us a power couple in California."

Like hell. Over my dead body.

Serena Weinstock comes from old wealth and a long line of senators. Her father just got inaugurated into office this term. Mother would love a marriage between Serena and me because it would give the family name more power in the legal world against the Statemans. Unfortunately for Mother, I will never marry Serena.

She's so fucking poisonous my dick would shrivel up and fall off after spending just one night with her.

I let out a chuckle while I slowly rise from my chair. Biting my bottom lip, I tilt my head, making sure there's a look of boredom on my face. "When I invest, I expect a return." I glance toward the stretch of beach, so it will bring the point across that even acknowledging her is a waste of my time, "Unfortunately, you're a depreciating asset."

Offended, she lifts her chin an inch. Her mouth pulls down at the corners, and it reminds me of my mother – haughty and pretentious.

Definitely not an attractive feature.

Before she can strike back at me, I begin to walk away. As I pass Grayson, my eyes flick to his and seeing the smirk on his face, I know this encounter with them will only be the first of many to come if we continue our vacation here.

"West, so kind of you to settle our tab," Mason says, and glancing over my shoulder, I see him shoving the folder with our bill against West's chest.

Wanting to save face with the rich and famous patrons seated around us, West painstakingly nods, although his eyes promise Mason retribution once they're back at the Academy.

With Mason and Lake following right behind me, we leave the rustic ambiance of the exclusive club.

"Are we leaving St. Tropez?" Lake asks once we're a good distance away from the club.

"Might as well." I glance at Mason. "Should we go home?"

"Hell no, I'm not spending my vacation anywhere near family." A frown still rests on his forehead. "Let's go to Hawaii. We haven't hit the waves in a long time."

I nod in agreement as we make our way back to the hotel. Taking my phone from my pocket, I call Stephanie, my father's personal assistant, and instruct her to make arrangements for our trip.

***

Earlier today, we returned to Montecito after spending the rest of our vacation in Hawaii. I take a deep breath before I walk into the dining room, knowing my family will already be seated for lunch.

12

Loosening the button on my tailor-made *Sanita* sport jacket from *Isaia*, I pull out a high-back chair and take a seat next to Julian, my older brother. Father's face is hidden behind the latest edition of the Financial Times. My eyes flick to Mother, who seems to be inspecting the dinner menu.

Thank God I'm leaving for the academy and won't have to endure another meal with my family for a while.

"Afternoon," I murmur in a low tone even though my greeting isn't needed. It's only a polite habit that's been ingrained into me since early childhood.

Since I got home, I kept myself busy with arrangements for the coming year, successfully avoiding my family members.

"What time are you leaving?" Mother asks, placing the menu down on the table and raising a well-manicured eyebrow at me.

Zero-interest in my life as always. It doesn't bother me. The less interest she shows, the better for me.

Clare Reyes, my mother for all intents and purposes, although she's never been motherly a day in her life, only cares about her image in the world of socialites.

"After lunch."

"Are you picking an assistant, seeing as it's your final year?" Julian asks. He sets his knife and fork down and lifting his chin higher, his dark eyes try to stare me down.

Julian sees me as a threat to his inheritance since Father dropped the gauntlet between us when he said whoever gets the best grades and works the hardest will take over as chairman once he retires.

I would've been happy to let Julian take the seat, but it's turned into a feud between us. My family is cold and calculative. There has never been love and affection between us. Don't get me wrong, we will stand together and fight as one if we come under attack, but once the threat has been dealt with, we go back to turning on each other.

"Yes." I keep my answer short, not wanting to spend more time than necessary at this table.

Where my mother is self-absorbed in her hunger to stay at the top as a socialite, Julian has only one goal in life – to keep me firmly beneath him so he can rule over our billion-dollar empire, CRC Holdings. He's never been good at sharing, and I know he'd rather die than share the company with me.

Father holds forty percent of the shares, and the remaining sixty is evenly divided between the Chargill and

Cutler families. Lake is the sole heir to Mr. Cutler's thirty percent, and after the tragic death of Mason's older sister, he became the sole heir to Mr. Chargill's wealth. I know this is a constant worry for Julian, seeing as both Mason and Lake are loyal to me. Even if Julian inherits thirty percent, leaving me with ten, I'll still have more power than him because I share an unbreakable bond with Mason and Lake.

Growing up, surrounded by power and wealth, has taught me one thing, paper is thicker than blood – specifically the paper with Woodrow Wilson's face printed on it, which is held in our family's security box at the bank. It was given to my grandfather as a gift and although it's worth was a hundred thousand dollars back in the nineteen hundred's, it's worth more than a million now. Whoever takes the Chairman seat will also inherit it.

"Please," Mother says, taking a heavy breath which breaks through my thoughts, "do give Serena special attention this year. Her father is a senator now, and she'd make a good asset to the family name."

Serena Weinstock. The perpetual thorn in my side.

When you're at the top of the food chain, relationships are mergers. Love is not a word we often use unless it's referring to an object.

"Also, make sure to greet Layla Shepard. She's Stephanie's daughter. Your father felt the need to be charitable by allowing her to study at Trinity." Mom's words are saturated in disdain, and her eyes shoot daggers at Father, who's still hiding behind the newspaper. The corners of her mouth pull down, making her look older than her forty-nine years.

It's no secret Mom doesn't approve of Stephanie Westwick. Father's personal assistant sees more of him than we do. Even though she's Father's PA, it falls under her list of responsibilities to make sure any personal problems the three founding families might have, get smoothed over, and the press never gets wind of it.

Knowing I'll get a reaction, I push my chair back and leave the plate of food untouched as I say, "Maybe I should make Layla my assistant. Keep it in the family."

It takes a lot of effort not to smile when Mother gasps, dropping her cutlery on the mahogany table.

"Don't you dare!" she yells after me as I leave the room. "Falcon!"

Walking through the ostentatious house, filled with enough riches to finance a small country, a grin spreads over my face. I adjust my suit jacket then pull my keys from my pocket as I walk out of the mansion to where my gunmetal-grey Lamborghini is parked. The *Lamborghini Veneno* was a gift for my twenty-first birthday and one of the few things I *love* in this world.

Just as I'm about to open the door, Julian grabs hold of my arm. I school my face into the usual bored expression before I glance at him.

"Personally, I don't care who you pick as your assistant, or what you do this year, as long as you don't put in any effort." The words are aloof, matching the hostile look in his eyes.

"As long as I'm not a threat to you, right?" I turn to face him, and you can almost feel the temperature drop as our cold gazes lock.

"Right. The seat is mine, and I won't have you get in my way of taking my rightful place."

Slightly tilting my head to the right, the corner of my mouth lifts in a sneer. "May the best man win," I whisper, my words laced with the promise that I'm not backing down anytime soon.

"I'll always be one step ahead of you," Julian hisses, and a muscle starts to jump in his jaw, showing just how much I'm getting to him.

I take a step closer, and being the same height as him, our eyes are at the same level. "And I'll be right behind you, so you better watch your back," leaning in until our breaths mingle, I bite the last word out, "Brother."

Chapter 1

Layla

Grabbing a seat in the middle of the auditorium, my gaze scans the group of first-year journalism students.

Nervous excitement fills the air, the kind you only feel on your first day of the rest of your life. Who you were in high school doesn't matter because college is a fresh start – new friends, new environment, new standards for what's acceptable and what's not.

The fact that I got a free ride to Trinity Academy because my mother is the personal assistant to Warren Reyes, CEO of CRC Holdings, is something I'll take to my grave. Mr. Reyes' father was one of the founding members of Trinity, a college meant for the rich and famous, which obviously doesn't include me.

Even though my mom gets paid a pretty decent income, and I've never wanted for anything in my life, it's not close to the wealth the other students come from – old money that's been built up over generations.

If they found out I'm not from the top one percent wealthy in the country, I'd be singled out, which is precisely what I want to avoid. I'm here to get my degree in journalism because it will go a long way in getting freelance jobs. It's my dream to join my dad and to travel the world with him.

A girl with long brown curls, classic features, and striking blue eyes takes the seat next to me. An eager grin spreads over her full mouth when she looks at me. "Kingsley Hunt. I have a 3.8 GPA and an out of control chocolate addiction."

Holding her slender hand out to me, she raises an expectant eyebrow.

"Layla Shepard. I hate wearing a bra and always change into my PJs as soon as I'm home," I say as I place my hand in hers.

"I like you." I'm surprised at the sincerity in her gaze as she bluntly admits this. "Let's be friends."

"Uhm… okay." Seeing as I don't know anyone else here, I figure I can use a friend, and Kingsley seems to be friendly.

A wave of murmurs washes over the auditorium, and I look to the front to see what all the commotion is about. Three guys walk onto the stage, each of their steps oozing with wealth and power. They each take a seat next to the podium with an air of grandeur one can only obtain from having infinite riches, making the chairs look like thrones.

Kingsley leans closer to me and whispers, "Their grandfathers are the founding members of the academy." Pointing to the guy nearest to the podium, she continues, "That's Lake Cutler."

Lake slouches in the chair, and resting his head back, he closes his eyes, as if our orientation day is taking away from his sleep. Light brown hair stands in every direction, with some sweeping over his forehead. With his features relaxed, he gives me the impression nothing in the world can bother him. Only confidence will allow you that kind of freedom to not care what others think of you.

"Lake's father is the vice-president of CRC Holdings." She stops, and looking at me asks, "You've heard of the company, right?'

Nodding, I answer, "Yeah."

"Oh, then I must be boring you with useless information," Kingsley laughs.

"Actually, I don't know much about them," I admit.

Mom never talks about her work with me. To be honest, that's putting it lightly. I hardly get to see Mom because she's either at the office or away on a business trip with Mr. Reyes.

"Cool, then I'll go on." Kingsley immediately proceeds by pointing at the guy next to Lake. "That's Mason Chargill."

The second I look at Mason, a shiver slithers down my spine, and every one of my alarms begin to go off. The guy looks like trouble with a capital T. There's a condescending smirk on his face, only adding to the menacing look courtesy of features that might as well have been carved from stone. Handsome... but the indifference and contempt rolling off his shoulders make him look threatening.

I'll be sure to avoid him at all costs.

"Mason's father is the president of the company. I heard Mason, Falcon, and Lake are studying to take over from their fathers, which makes sense seeing as the three of them are the heirs to CRC Holdings."

When Kingsley doesn't continue, I ask, "So the third guy is Falcon Reyes?" Mom told me to be on my best behavior because Mr. Reyes' youngest son is a senior here at the academy, but I've never met any of them in person.

Now that I know what the heirs look like, it will make it easier to avoid them.

"Oh, yeah. Sorry, I got stuck on Mason," she admits with a grin. "I could stare at him all day long."

My eyes drift over the guys before stopping at Falcon. My first impression of Falcon is no better than the one I have of Mason. With a sharp, intelligent look, he reeks of arrogance wrapped in an icy layer of indifference.

He lifts his chin and glances in my direction as if he can feel my eyes on him. From across the auditorium, our eyes lock, and every muscle in my body tenses as an unnerving feeling ripples over me. There are easily ten rows of chairs between Falcon and me, yet his cold gaze has the power to make me feel like I've just been singled out. His shoulders are set square, commanding and formidable, giving me the impression he's the leader of the three.

Breaking eye-contact, I slide down in my chair and hide behind the guy sitting right in front of me.

Yeah, definitely gonna stay away from Falcon.

"Falcon's father is the CEO and chairman of CRC Holdings." Kingsley lets out a sigh. "With the kind of wealth they come from, they might be gorgeous to look at but deadly to play with."

"That, my friend, I one hundred percent agree with."

23

The introduction begins, and all the students quiet down. I usually pride myself in paying attention, but today, I find myself zoning out as my eyes get stuck on the three men sitting up front.

Sometimes I wonder what it would be like to have such wealth – not having to worry about your bank account ever running on fumes.

Deep in thought, my eyes leave them only to jump from one student to the next. Most are wearing watches I've never seen before, making my TAG Heuer look like a pavement special. It's not like I'm into the latest fashion and luxury brands, but coming to this college, you quickly notice it's what sets you apart from the rest of the students.

Once the introduction is over, we all file out of the auditorium and into the bright California sunlight.

"Which building are you staying in?" Kingsley asks as we walk over the well-maintained green lawn toward the residence section.

I scrunch my nose because I think the names for the buildings are lame. "I'm staying in the Hope Diamond. What's with the weird names for the buildings?" I ask, hoping Kingsley will be able to tell me more.

Instead, her eyes widen, and she grabs my arm. "You're so lucky! How did you manage to get a room in *their* building?"

"Their building?" I ask, raising an eyebrow.

"The penthouse belongs to Falcon, Mason, and Lake. Usually, only other business partners can get a suite in the Hope Diamond."

I blink as she overly excited rambles, and once I find my bearings, I mumble, "It makes no difference to me where I stay."

I hope she doesn't ask about my family because I'd hate to lie to her, but there's no way I'm trusting her with my secret only minutes after meeting her.

"Well, you're lucky. Your family must be business partners with CRC then?" Kingsley asks the question I've been dreading most.

"Something like that," I skirt around the truth, hoping it won't come back to bite me in the ass.

I know for a fact Mom being Mr. Reyes' personal assistant won't mean shit to the other students and might make me a target, which is the last thing I need.

We walk toward the dorms that look like five-star hotels instead of student housing.

"I'm in the Pink Star, which is the building opposite yours. The Oppenheimer Blue is the third building."

"Why the names?" I repeat my question from earlier.

"They're ranked according to the most expensive stones. Depending on where your family falls on the wealth ladder, you get assigned to a room in the appropriate building. The Oppenheimer Blue is where you'll find the millionaires next door or the capitalist class. If you're from one of the ruling fifteen thousand families in the States or glittering rich like my family, you're in the Pink Star. Only those on the Forbes 400 list make it past the doors of the Hope Diamond."

Shaking my head, I let out a sigh, "Ridiculous if you ask me. I'm going to have to research all these things, so I don't step on any toes."

"I'll make you a list of the important stuff," Kingsley offers.

"That would be great."

We part ways at the entrance to the Hope Diamond, agreeing to meet in an hour for an early dinner.

Walking into the luxurious building, the marble floors gleam under extravagant chandeliers. My shoulders sag, and I lose a little of the excitement from being able to study here.

My dad is a gypsy at heart, and since the divorce, he's never stayed in one place for long. I love both my parents, but I take after Dad. Material things have never mattered to me, and now I'm in a college with people who only care about status, power, and money.

Damn, it sucks.

I should've insisted on attending a regular college, but Mom was so excited I couldn't let her down.

Sliding the card through the electronic lock, I step into my suite. I glance around the space then look out the window at the perfect view of the hills. I love the Ojai Valley, where Trinity Academy is situated. The hills surrounding the campus are gorgeous.

"You can fool everyone for four years," I mumble, not quite believing the words myself. "Just don't stand out in any way, and no one will notice you."

Chapter 2

Falcon

Having to attend all the introduction ceremonies on the first day is mind-numbingly boring.

"I miss the waves already," Lake mumbles, not happy about being back at the academy. "The gap year we took after school was the best. We had no worries back then. Shit, it feels like a lifetime ago."

"Yeah, waking up whenever we wanted. No nagging parents. None of this shit at the academy," Mason reminisces. "Only us and the ocean."

"Those were good times," I agree, feeling a little nostalgic myself. After graduating, we spent the entire year traveling while searching for the biggest and best waves to surf. Leaving the heavy burden of our family names behind, there was no set schedule to follow.

"Remind me again why we're here?" Lake grumbles.

Mason lets out a deep chuckle. "My father threatened to freeze our accounts if we didn't get our asses back to reality."

"Right. I can't wait until you take over from him." Lake wags his eyebrows playfully at Mason.

"Yeah? You think I won't freeze your ass if you don't work?" Mason kids with him.

"And you call yourself my friend," Lake huffs but then adds. "Falcon will take care of me." He catches up to where I'm walking a step ahead of them and throws his arm around my shoulders. "Right? You'd never let me starve."

I grin at their bantering and shrug Lake's arm off. "I'd go bankrupt if I have to feed you. You're a bottomless-fucking-pit."

Pretending to look hurt, Lake places a hand over his heart. "Damn. So cold, brother." He shakes his head at me then glances in the direction of the restaurant we're headed toward. "Can't help I have a healthy appetite."

"There's nothing healthy about the amount of pizza you can consume," Mason gives his opinion as we step into the restaurant.

Some students instantly scatter out of our way. Around here, the top one percent is made up of the three founding families, which are Mason, Lake, and myself. I have to admit, in the beginning having this kind of power was both incredible and addictive, but as the years passed, it became tedious, leaving a stale taste in my mouth.

The academy is structured, so we'll build connections and get a taste of what the real business world will be like. Everyone here has an agenda, and befriending the three of us is at the top of their lists. With us being in our final year, we each get to pick an assistant. It's a huge thing being chosen as one of our assistants. It means you're good enough to be singled out by us, which gives you an automatic rise in status. It's a known fact that if you have one of us as a connection, you'll be set for life, which makes us practically gods.

Little do they know Lake and I aren't sure whether we'll be joining the family business. Right now, Mason is the only one of the three of us who will be working at the company. Lake mentioned he'd like to open up a café in Europe. He's been looking into studying as a barista in Italy once he's finished studying Law.

I've been playing around on the stock market and have been pretty lucky. With the funds I've managed to make on my own, I'm thinking of opening a business where I can help inventors bring their creations to life. That way my degree in Intellectual Property LLB will come in handy.

Nudging me with his arm, Lake draws my attention. "Isn't that Stephanie's daughter?"

I glance at the girl Lake is looking at, and from the inexpensive labeled capris, sandals, and plain blue t-shirt, it's clear she doesn't belong here. She stands out like a sore thumb amongst all the other girls with their exclusive brand clothing and accessories.

"Since when does Trinity give scholarships?" Mason asks, his gaze filled with boredom as he spares the table Layla is seated at a glance.

Not just anyone can get into Trinity. Every single student here comes from a wealthy background.

"She's my father's latest charity case," I answer. She has guts coming here because once the other students realize she's not from a wealthy family, shit will hit the fan. For a split-second, I feel a twinge of worry, but it quickly fades.

Murmurs fill the air as we walk to our table. I take my usual seat and glancing to my left I watch as Serena stops at the table where Layla is seated with a group of first-year students.

I frown as I take a closer look at Layla. I expected her to have black hair like Stephanie, but she must take after her father's side. Silky blonde hair is caught in a ponytail,

31

and she's not wearing much makeup. Her fair complexion makes her look feminine and flawless.

Yeah, even I will admit she's beautiful, which means she's going to attract a lot of unwanted attention.

They're gonna see right through her. She doesn't stand a chance.

"She's not going to last long," Mason gives his opinion while looking over the menu.

A waitress comes to our table, and while Lake orders an obscene amount of food, my eyes drift back to where Serena is talking to Layla.

Just then, Grayson and West enter the restaurant and spotting Serena, they make their way over to her.

"Serena, introduce me to your new friend," Grayson says loud enough for half the restaurant to hear.

"I was just greeting Kingsley," Serena quickly corrects Grayson. "I couldn't be bothered with the other freshmen."

Grayson grins at Serena. "Yeah, you better keep Kingsley close. You wouldn't want her father's hand to slip while he's working on your face."

"Layla, let's go grab dinner off-campus. I suddenly lost my appetite," Kingsley says as she gets up from her chair.

Layla stands up, but Grayson takes a couple of steps closer and blocks her way.

"Don't run off before we've had a chance to meet." He smiles broadly, and interest flickers across his features. "I'm Grayson Stateman."

Layla ignores the hand stretched out to her. "Layla Shepard. It's nice meeting you, but if you'll excuse…"

Slowly, Grayson shakes his head, not getting out of her way. "You're not excused. Sit down."

"She's not at your beck and call, Grayson," Kingsley snaps, making a slow grin form around my lips.

Gotta give Kingsley points for standing up for Layla.

Seeing an opportunity to remind Grayson I hold all the power here at Trinity, I slowly rise from my seat. There's also the fact that the bastard always had a hard time understanding the word no, so I'll be doing the girl a favor for which she'll owe me.

Hearing Mason and Lake get up behind me, I know they have my back as I walk over to Layla. I come up behind her and meeting Grayson's eyes over the top of her head, the corner of my mouth lifts.

I let out a sigh. "Grovelling for attention again?"

The smile fades from Grayson's face, and his mouth sets in a grim line. "Interfering in other people's business again?"

Layla glances over her shoulder, and when her eyes land on me, they widen, and she quickly takes a step to the side so she can see both Grayson and me.

I watch as her shoulders stiffen before she wets her lips, and for some reason, it bugs the hell out of me when the movement catches Grayson's eye.

Her brown eyes dart to Grayson before coming back to my face. Our eyes lock, and I'm caught off guard when I see the uneasy look in them. "Falcon."

She looks uncomfortable being in my presence, and it makes me wonder how much has Stephanie told her daughter about me.

"Mother said you'd be joining Trinity," I say, and a second later, shocked gasps fill the air from the students watching us. I'm fully aware it's because everyone now thinks I know Layla on a personal level.

Fuck, I have no idea why I just did that.

"Do you know each other?" I hear Serena's voice as it hits a high pitch. Ignoring her shocked reaction, I look back to Grayson.

He lets out a chuckle, lightly shaking his head. "Am I supposed to read between the lines?"

Glad he took the bait, I shrug. "Make of it what you want."

"Uhm…" Layla fidgets, tucking some hair behind her ear. "It was nice meeting everyone, but I'm just going to squeeze past and be on my way."

I take a step to the right so she can get by me, but Grayson's hand shoots out, and he grabs hold of her arm.

"Why the hurry? We were getting to know each other before we were so rudely interrupted."

He pulls Layla back toward him, which makes her stumble, but before I can react, she manages to regain her balance.

A frown forms on her forehead, and her eyes fill with a defiant look.

As much as I'd like to see whether she can stand up for herself, I'm not willing to pass on the opportunity to put Grayson in his place.

The words are low and carry a silent threat when I demand, "Let go of her arm."

"Why? It's not like she's your property. You don't own everything at Trinity," Grayson taunts. He widens his eyes, pretending to be shocked as he mocks me. "Wow, can you believe that? There's actually something you don't have."

Fucker.

Before I can think things through, the words leave my mind. "I've chosen her as my assistant."

Layla's head snaps to me, and the defiant look in her eyes darkens. "Excuse me?"

Gasps fill the air around us, followed by more shocked murmurs. I feel the wave of disappointment as it spreads through the students who all had hopes to get the coveted position.

Layla yanks her arm free from Grayson's hold and scowls at me. "I'm not interested in being your assistant." Her words are bold and fearless, and it actually makes me admire her a little.

Mason chuckles behind me, clearly enjoying the show.

"It's not your choice to make," I say, and needing to put Layla in her place, I take a step closer to her. I lean in until our cheeks brush, and whisper so only she will hear, "I'm sure you learned a thing or two from your mother, so don't disappoint me, Shepard. You have some big shoes to fill, and I'd hate for your mother's image to suffer because of you."

She inhales sharply as I pull back, and sparing her a don't-fuck-with-me smile, I direct my attention back to Grayson.

"It's settled then," I state, bringing this conversation to a close now that I've reminded Grayson of how powerless he is.

"If you think just because she's your assistant, she's off-limits to me, you're mistaken. It will only make it so much sweeter when I win."

I let out a burst of laughter. "Stateman, are you actually trying to compete with me right now?"

Whispers spread out around us, only making my smile widen.

'Does Grayson have a death wish?'

'Oh my God, I can't believe what I'm seeing.'

'Falcon's going to destroy him.'

'Idiot. It's his funeral.'

Grayson must also hear them because his face turns red with embarrassment and anger.

"I've heard enough," Layla almost grinds the words out, clearly not impressed by the showdown between Grayson and me.

Before Grayson can do anything stupid, or at least more idiotic than he already has, Lake moves past me.

"Chill, guys. You're going to give me an ulcer if you carry on like this the entire year." Lake takes Layla's hand, and he pulls her away from us.

Now that Layla is out of the way, my eyes rest cold on Grayson.

"Lucky for you, Lake stepped in," Grayson sneers. His eyes dart past me to where Mason is before he takes a step back. "Let's go," he says to West and Serena, who have silently been watching.

"Things just got interesting here at Trinity. I might actually enjoy this year," Mason murmurs.

Chapter 3

Layla

I'm feeling all kinds of confused as I let Lake drag me out of the restaurant.

"Damnit, their timing sucks," he grumbles under his breath. "Just as they were about to bring my order."

"Thanks, Lake, you're a lifesaver," Kingsley says as she catches up with us where we've come to a stop on the lawn.

My mind is still reeling from everything that just happened in the restaurant. So much for flying under the radar. Thanks to those two idiots, it feels like a spotlight has illuminated my being here.

Talking about idiots…

My gaze locks with Falcon's as he and Mason walk toward us. Back at the restaurant, when I turned around and saw Falcon standing behind me, I almost had a heart attack. Earlier at orientation, Falcon was sitting a distance from me. Seeing him so up close was damn unnerving. He is too good-looking, too intense, and way too intimidating.

Falcon stops next to Lake and giving me a bored look, his words are coated with arrogance as he says, "You're welcome by the way."

Normally, I can't read people's faces to save my life. But Falcon's eyes... they're alert, intelligent, and so damn alive.

Feigning indifference, I roll my eyes. The last thing I need right now is for Falcon to know how unsettled I feel by him. "I never asked for your help in the first place." Not wanting to come across as being rude, I reluctantly add, "But... thank you."

The corner of his mouth twitches slightly before his features return to their unyielding state. "You start as my assistant tomorrow. Don't disappoint me."

Feeling frustrated and irritable, a wave of heat creeps up my neck and face. "Oh no, hold on! I never agreed to be your assistant." Needing to make it clear to him that I have zero interest in the position, I continue, "I don't want to be your assistant. Get one of the other students. I'm pretty sure there's a long line of applicants who would love the honor." When he just smirks at me, I add, "I'm just here to study. Pick someone else."

To my dismay, the smirk around his full lips only keeps growing. "You don't get a choice in the matter. You start tomorrow morning at eight. Don't be late." He starts to turn away, then stops and glancing at me one last time, he adds, "Coffee. Two sugars. Cream."

My mind races for the perfect come back, but before I can form the words, Falcon walks away, leaving me staring at the back of his broad shoulders.

"What the hell just happened?" I whisper, shaking my head to rid myself of the confusion. Tearing my eyes away from Falcon, I look to Kingsley. "It feels like I stepped into the twilight zone."

Kingsley shrugs. "We survived." She lets out a nervous burst of laughter. "That's all I care about." Letting out a deep breath, she repeats, "We survived." A smile forms on her face, and her eyes begin to sparkle. "But you have to admit, that was exciting."

Immediately I begin to shake my head. "Girl, no. There was nothing exciting about that."

The nerve of that idiot telling me to be his assistant. Just watch me. I'm going to do my best to be epically bad at this assistant thing.

I glance over my shoulder to make sure no one is watching before I reach for the salt. With a rebellious grin all over my face, I stir the salt into the coffee, then try to school my face into a careless look. Picking up the cup, I struggle not to laugh as I walk over to where Falcon is sitting with his friends.

Mason notices me first and says something which makes Falcon glance in my direction. For a split-second, I feel nervous, and I'm just about to hesitate when an arrogant grin tugs at the left corner of Falcon's mouth.

Nope, I'm doing this. I'm going to show him I won't be messed with.

Placing the cup in front of Falcon, I smile as sweetly as I can manage. "Your coffee, Sir."

Feeling Falcon's eyes on me, I take a deep breath before I meet them. Again, I feel the punch to my gut from making eye contact with him.

Scared he'll see right through my act, I turn away from the table. "Enjoy."

It takes a lot of effort to not run from the restaurant, and even more to not peek over my shoulder to see his reaction once he tastes the coffee.

Darting out the door, I turn left and rush to where I can hide behind the wall so I can peek through the windows. Slowly, I inch forward until I have a view of Falcon, and a wide smile splits over my face as I watch him pick up the cup. When he takes a sip, an anxious squeak rushes up my throat.

When a smile forms on Falcon's face as he looks down at the cup, a frown begins to form on my forehead. Shaking his head slightly, he sets it back down on the table.

"That's it? All the trouble, and he just smiles?" Letting out a disappointed sigh, I inch back behind the wall.

"Why are you standing here?"

Kingsley's voice has me jumping with fright. Swinging around, I slap a hand over my chest. "You'll give me a damn heart attack, woman."

Kingsley leans to the side and glancing into the restaurant she tries to see what I was looking at. "What were you looking at?"

"Nothing." The word bursts from me, and I quickly grab her hand to pull her away. Walking toward the office, I change the subject. "Let's go get our class schedules."

We're making our way back toward the dorms, aka palaces fit for royalty, when we cross paths with Grayson and Serena.

"Kingsley, let's go for coffee." The way Serena talks makes it sound like an order instead of an invitation. She gives me a side glance, then continues, "We didn't have time to catch up yesterday."

Kingsley gives me a questioning look, which has me sputtering, "Sure, go ahead. I'll see you later."

I'm just about to start walking away when Grayson takes a step to the right, blocking me in the same way he did the day before. "Don't run away. Join us."

Another order? Geez, don't these people know how to ask nicely?

"Yeah, come." Kingsley hooks her arm through mine and gives me a pleading look. "Please."

Why have coffee with people you don't like? Biting back the question on the tip of my tongue, I nod and let her pull me toward the restaurant, desperately hoping Falcon isn't still there.

When we sit down, Grayson takes the seat next to me and then proceeds to scoot his chair closer to mine. Having very little self-control left, I roll my eyes and purposely look at Kingsley.

A tug at my hair has me scowling as my eyes snap to Grayson.

"You're hurting my pride," he pouts.

"I don't care about your pride." The words are out before I can filter them.

"Ouch, that's cold, babe." There's something about the smile on his face that makes me feel uncomfortable, and I move my chair closer to Kingsley's and farther away from his.

"I don't blame her. It's not like you inspire any warmth, Grayson."

When I hear Mason's voice, I glance over my shoulder so fast, I almost sprain my neck in the process. Seeing Falcon and Lake with him, my heart sinks to my little toe.

"Let's not start something again," Serena drawls with a bored tone. As soon as her eyes land on Falcon, she pouts. "We should have dinner tonight. We have a lot to discuss."

My eyes dart back to Falcon, and I watch as he takes a deep breath. Lifting a hand to his face, he brushes his middle finger over his eyebrow. "Yeah, that's never going to happen."

My head swings back to Serena, and it's beginning to feel like I'm watching a tennis match.

Serena's eyes narrow, and her mouth turns down at the corners. "I don't think your mother will be very pleased to hear how rude you are to me."

As my head turns back to where Falcon is, I actually hear the click right before a burning pain engulfs my neck. "Ahh! Crap."

"Yeah, we should leave," Kingsley states, taking advantage of the moment to get out of here. She gets up, then reaches for my arm.

"No, wait," I almost whimper the words as the burning sensation is joined by a sharp ache underneath my right ear. "I just pulled a muscle." I let out a soft groan as I carefully raise my hand to my neck, so I can support my head.

"Seriously? This is not the time, nor the place to put on an act," Serena snaps.

Not having the energy, I ignore her snarky comment and slowly begin to get up from the chair.

"Let's go to the nurse's office. Maybe she'll have something we can put on your neck to relax the muscle," Kingsley says as she takes hold of my left arm to help me into a standing position.

"It's torture just watching you stand up," Falcon growls.

Before I know what's happening, an arm hooks under my knees and another wraps around the middle of my back. I let out a squeak as the movement of Falcon picking me up jars my body, causing another flash of hot pain to engulf the back of my head. Letting go of my neck, I slap Falcon against the chest as I scowl up at him.

"Slowly, Falcon," Kingsley gasps.

"You want to carry her?" he snaps at Kingsley.

With my eyes wide, and the up-close view I have of his jaw, my body and mind freeze.

"I'll carry her," Grayson offers, snaping me right out of the shocked state I was caught in.

At the same time, Falcon growls the word, it explodes over my lips, "No."

When the students in the restaurant all look at us, I begin to sputter, "I mean… uhm… I… I can walk. There's nothing wrong with my legs."

Falcon lets out an impatient breath through his nose and his arms tense under me. Without another word, he stalks toward the doors, and as soon as we're outside, he grumbles, "You could help a little. It's not like you weigh nothing."

I glare up at him as I wrap my arms around his neck, resisting the temptation to strangle him. "It's not like I asked you to carry me," I snap back.

Glancing down at me, a sexy smirk pulls at the corner of his mouth.

Don't give me that sexy smirk, thinking it will make me swoon.

As if the jerk can hear my thoughts, the grin keeps growing.

Stop it. I'm not going to fall for it.

By the time Falcon has a smile plastered all over his too-hot-to-handle face, I'm swallowing hard on the attraction I feel.

Dropping my eyes to his neck, I hope to the high heavens Falcon didn't see any of the emotions on my face.

When we reach the nurse's office, my heart is beating out of control, and I'm beginning to sweat from all the effort it's taking to not look at the stupid handsome face right above me.

Falcon puts me down on a bed, and instead of pulling back, he places his hands on the mattress, effectively caging me.

When he leans a little down and catches my eyes, I feel a wave of excitement and attraction crash over me.

"What?" I wanted to snap at him, but the word comes out sounding way too breathless.

Don't fail me, heart.

Not this man.

Not ever.

"Thank. You." He pronounces the words slowly with a low, gravelly timbre.

"For what?" I ask, feeling confused, desperate, and like I'm about to overheat all at once.

Letting out a chuckle, Falcon shakes his head as he finally pulls back. "Would it kill you to just say thank you?"

"Huh?" Frowning, my frazzled mind scrambles to catch up to the moment from where it was stuck in intoxicated-by-hot-dude-land. As common sense returns to me, heat creeps up my neck.

He's just a pretty face, Layla. This is Falcon Reyes we're talking about. Off-limits. Mom's future boss. Heir to wealth beyond your wildest imagination. Falling for him will just be plain stupid.

"Thank you." Lucky for me, the nurse comes in right then, saving me from being alone with Falcon for another torturous second.

Dressed in a pristine navy-blue uniform, the woman looks more like a PA than a nurse. "Mr. Reyes, is everything okay?" she asks him, not even looking at me.

"Layla seems to have sprained her neck," he offers the information.

"How did it happen?" she asks as she moves closer to me so she can take a look.

"By being too nosy," Falcon states, and before I can even glare at the jerk, he turns around and walks out.

———

It's only been four days since classes started and I'm already swamped with assignments. Thanks to some painkillers and stretching exercises, my neck is all better.

I overslept this morning and didn't have time for breakfast, which has my stomach growling as I walk to the restaurant to meet Kingsley for lunch.

Sitting down, I let out a sigh while placing my bag on the floor next to my chair.

"I could eat half a cow right now," I admit, giving Kingsley a smile.

"That makes two of us. Let's order."

After the waiter leaves with our order, Kingsley leans back in her chair and lets out a groan. "How are we going to get all this work done?" She shoots forward and looks hopefully at me. "You think it's too late to change my major?"

Chuckling, I shake my head. "To what? Everyone is complaining about their workload no matter what they're studying."

She slumps back again and pouts. "True. It sucks."

"You can say that again."

"What sucks?"

Both our heads snap up when Lake comes to stand next to our table.

Gentle with the neck, Layla. Let's not sprain the damn thing again so soon after getting it healed.

Kingsley grabs Lake's hand and pulls him closer to the table. "Sit! You're just the person I'm looking for."

"I am?" Lake asks while grabbing the seat next to her. The waiter brings our order of pizzas, and as he places it down on the table, Lake grins. "Just in time."

"Should I bring your milkshake to this table?" the waiter asks.

"That would be great, Jeremy." I find myself staring at Lake when he smiles at the waiter before he proceeds to help himself to a couple of slices.

Kingsley's laughter draws my attention to her, and seeing that she's laughing at me, I ask, "What?"

"The look on your face is priceless."

"What look?"

"You're looking at Lake as if he's an alien."

"The way he eats, I wouldn't be surprised," Mason comments. He takes a seat next to Lake, and it has my eyes widening.

Shit.

No.

Oh hell.

Please.

"We're having pizza? Again?" Falcon complains as he sits down in the only open chair, which happens to be next to me.

Ugh.

Last time I'm praying.

"*We're* having pizza," I answer while I quickly grab three slices before it's all gone. I shove the greasy yumminess into my mouth and let out a moan as I begin to chew.

Food. Finally.

"And now I understand the meaning of food porn." Mason's words stun the hell out me and trying to swallow too fast, I almost kill myself by choking.

While I cough, Kingsley gently pats my back.

Mason lets out a disgruntled breath and shaking his head, he reaches for a slice of pizza, muttering, "Totally ruined the fantasy for me."

As soon as I can breathe properly, I glare at Mason, "And you're totally ruining lunch for me."

When my eyes collide with his dark ones, an apprehensive shiver skitters down my spine.

Laaayyyylllaaaa! When are you going to learn to shut up? Do you have a death wish?

"She didn't have breakfast this morning," Kingsley quickly jumps in, trying to save my butt by making an excuse for me.

"Falcon," Mason growls, still keeping his eyes locked with mine, "your assistant doesn't know her place."

Yeah, so much for having any survival instincts.

Taking a deep breath, I open my mouth to let Mason know what I think about his comment but instead swallow a gulp of air which goes down the wrong hole when Falcon places his arm around my shoulders.

This time it's not Kingsley gently patting my back as I almost cough up a lung, but Falcon slapping my back. When I clear my throat, I glare at him. "You can stop now. I'm breathing again."

He gives me one last slap right between my shoulder blades then brings his hand up to the back of my neck. Feeling his fingers wrap around my neck makes a different kind of shiver rush down my spine from when I made eye contact with Mason.

The shivers quickly up and vanish when he pulls me closer and locking eyes with me, he says, "It's hard to believe you're Ste..."

Before Falcon can finish his sentence, I shoot up out of the chair and grabbing his hand, I pull him behind me as I rush from the restaurant.

Making sure there's no one close to us who can accidentally overhear, I stop and spin around while hissing, "Can you please keep it a secret? I don't want anyone here knowing who my mother is."

Falcon actually looks stunned by my sudden actions. "Why?"

I glance around again, just to be sure, and taking a step closer to Falcon, I whisper, "Can you imagine what the other students will do to me if they found out I'm your employee's daughter?"

Falcon leans a little closer, and whispers, "Oh yeah, I didn't think about that. So we're going to keep it a secret?"

"Yes."

The fleeting feeling of relief from thinking Falcon understood where I was coming from disappears the second the corner of his mouth lifts. "Nothing in this world is free. You better up your game at being my assistant if you want me to keep my mouth shut."

Ass.

"Why do I have to be your assistant?" I ask, a miserable feeling sinking into my gut.

"Because I say so," he states. When I notice the tiny golden flecks in his deep brown eyes, I realize how close we're standing to each other.

I quickly take a step back to put some distance between us while my traitorous cheeks begin to glow with embarrassment. "That's not a reason," I mumble.

"In my world it is."

Not wanting my secret getting out, I let out a miserable sigh and ask, "What do I have to do as your assistant?"

"For starters, I like my coffee without salt."

My eyes dart up to Falcon's, and seeing the gloating look on his face, I can't stop myself from scowling. "Fine, no salt."

"Give me your phone."

"Why?" Reluctantly, I pull it from my pocket.

Falcon doesn't answer me but instead takes it from me and proceeds to dial his own number. Handing it back to me, he says, "When I call, you answer. If I request something via text message, you do it. It's as simple as that."

I scrunch my nose as I grudgingly program his number into my phone.

"Layla." Hearing him say my name has me forgetting about the phone, and my eyes rushing to meet his. The serious look on his face throws me for a loop and dries all the spit from my mouth. "I might find your sassy attitude entertaining but watch what you say to Mason. He has a short temper, and you don't want him losing it."

Understanding the warning, I nod. "Okay." I'm not going to argue about that. I find Mason scary, and if Falcon is taking the time to warn me, I figure I should listen.

"Get your butt back into the restaurant and eat. I don't want to hear I'm starving you."

Falcon leaves me standing with my lips parted and eyes wide.

He actually sounded caring.

Yeah… right.

Chapter 4

Falcon

Getting up from the desk I'm occupying in the library, I struggle to suppress the grin as I walk to where Layla is standing on her toes, stretching herself as far as she can to try and get the book I requested.

I come up behind her, and reaching over her, I grab hold of the book. Layla glances up at me from over her shoulder, and for a moment, her eyes widen before her face sets into the scowl I'm getting used to seeing on her.

"Seriously, Falcon, you could've just done it yourself in the first place. I have assignments to finish, as well."

When she tries to duck to the left, and away from me, my hand darts out and settles on her hip. I'm surprised by my actions, but it doesn't stop me from taking a step closer to her.

The scowl vanishes from her face and is quickly replaced by a shocked look.

Our eyes meet, and I feel a foreign sensation ripple through my chest. Confused by the emotion and wanting to save face, I lean down and whisper, "But it's more fun watching you get all riled up."

Layla's lips part and I hear her take a sharp breath. A smile splits over my face when she brings her hands up between us, pushing me back. "That's because you're an ass."

When she walks away from me, a chuckle rumbles up my throat. I watch her take the seat where her laptop is. She lets out a sigh and shakes her head before she reads over the work she's done already.

This girl.

No one would dare talk to me the way she does, and it makes all the difference. She's feisty, which feels like a breath of fresh air in the staleness my life has become.

Walking back to my own desk, the thought nibbles at me... *Yeah, but if Serena or any other girl tried talking to you like that, you'd be angry. It's not just because Layla is feisty... it's more.*

Shaking the thought off, I sit down and focus on my work.

Thirty minutes later, my phone starts to vibrate. When I see Mother's name flashing on the screen, I let out an exasperated breath. Knowing she'll keep calling until I answer, I close my laptop and quickly shove it into my bag. Getting up, I hitch the strap of the bag over my shoulder and walk toward the exit.

"Mother," I answer once I'm close to the doors. I step outside into the sunlight and start back in the direction of the dorms.

"Falcon, why do you insist on disobeying me every chance you get?"

With my free hand, I pinch the bridge of my nose, so I don't lose my shit. Fighting with my mother is a waste of time.

"What did I do this time?" I ask, so I'll at least know what this damn call is about.

"I asked you to give special attention to Serena. I just came from a luncheon with Mrs. Weinstock and had to listen to how rude you've been to her daughter. We need this merger with Senator Weinstock's family." From the ire in her voice, I can just picture how red her face must be right now.

"You didn't ask me to do anything," I remind her. "You instructed me, and we both know I don't like being told what to do."

The sharp intake of breath coming over the line has me glancing up at the heavens for strength. I'm so tired of doing this dance with my family. If it's not one thing, it's another.

"You need to grow up, Falcon. You're turning twenty-three in a couple of weeks. How can you expect us to trust you with the business when you act like a child?"

"Mother," I grind the word out as I struggle to hold onto the last of my patience, "why don't you start by admitting the truth? You expect me to marry the woman of your choosing, to better your social status. This merger, as you like to refer to it, has nothing to do with the wellbeing of the business, or with my life." Saying the truth out loud feels freeing, and it encourages me to continue, "I will never bind myself to a woman like Serena. The sooner you accept it, the better."

Heavy breaths are all I hear for a couple of seconds before Mother hisses, "I will not stand for this behavior! It's unacceptable, and your father will hear of this."

The call cuts, letting an empty silence hang around me.

I come to a stop midway to the dorm, and closing my eyes, I take a deep breath. A bitter taste fills my mouth as the familiar desolate feeling swamps my chest.

If it weren't for Lake and Mason, I would've ended my life by now. Besides them, there's nothing good in my life.

Wealth. Power. Status.

Those words only suck the meager life out of my worthless existence.

I know it makes me sound ungrateful, but damn, it's suffocating and unfulfilling living a life that's been mapped out from birth to death. Every word spoken is calculated, and I can only align myself with people who will add to my wealth and status.

Really? Is this life? Am I going to end up a replica of my mother and father?

Fuck no.

Please, no.

There has to be more to life.

"Falcon." Hearing Layla's voice behind me, I quickly take a deep breath, so none of the emotions warring inside of me shows on my face.

Layla walks up beside me, then slams a book into my chest. My hand automatically flies up to keep the book from falling when she lets go of it.

"I checked it out for you, so you won't bother me later to go get it again." She sounds annoyed, and it only ignites my own irritation.

Taking a step to the side, I move into her personal space. When our eyes meet, it feels as if an electric current passes between us.

"Shepard, you better start watching how you talk to me. Your little show of attitude might have been entertaining at first, but I'm quickly growing bored with it. Know your place. Testing my patience is the last thing you want to do."

The brown of her eyes darkens, making her skin look paler. "Show of attitude?" Clenching her jaw, she also takes a step closer and lifting her chin, she gives me a daring look. "I will not allow anyone to walk over me, least of all you. I'm not here to be at your beck and call. I'm here to study."

I'm filled with a weird sense of satisfaction by Layla fighting back, which spurs me on. Shoving the book back against her chest, my voice drops low as I say, "You get to study because I'm paying for it. One snap of my fingers and you're out." Stepping around her, I add, "Take the book back. I no longer need it."

"A... F... I can't... what the hell... ass," I hear her stammer behind me.

I have to admit, I feel a hell of a lot better after the encounter with Layla. It's as if just being around her helps me to stay grounded.

Walking into The Hope Diamond, I go to stand in front of the elevators. While waiting for the doors to open, I mutter, "I needed that damn book."

―――――――――――――――――――――

I'm not going to lie, I'm exhausted after the past week. I've just finished the last class for today and purposely ignore students either greeting me or saying something to get my attention. Right now, I just want to get back to my suite so I can sleep.

Not wanting to get stuck in an elevator with the other students, I head down the stairs. Taking the last step, I turn left toward the exit and almost collide with the janitor as he hauls cleaning supplies out of a maintenance closet.

"Sorry, Mr. Reyes. I didn't see you there." The elderly man quickly shoves the door closed before he shuffles away from me.

With my eyes still on the man, I take a step forward and again come to a sudden halt when someone bumps into me.

"Crap!" The hushed word has me glancing down as annoyance begins to bubble inside of me. I'm met with Layla's face, a panicked look tightening her features.

"What's wrong?" The words burst from me, and I feel a twinge of worry.

Layla glances over her shoulder, then lets out a little squeak before she tries to dart around me. I grab hold of her arm to keep her from running off while my eyes scan over the entrance to find the reason for her panic.

"Not now, Falcon. I'm trying to avoid Grayson and Serena," she snaps.

"Serena?" Just then, my eyes land on them as they come into the building. "Shit." Serena is the absolute last person I have the energy for right now.

Not thinking twice, I yank open the door to the maintenance closet, and after shoving Layla in, I quickly step inside.

When I pull the door shut behind us, we're plunged into darkness. Layla takes a step away from me and knocks into something on the floor. It all happens so fast, but before I can move a muscle, Layla lets out another squeak, and then her hand connects with my chest. She grabs a fistful of my shirt and ends up plastering herself against me.

For a moment, we both stand frozen. Clearing her throat, Layla shuffles backward. I bring my arms up and grabbing hold of her shoulders, I pull her back against me.

"Stop moving." The words come out in a low grumble. "You're the worst person to hide with."

Her hair tickles my chin, and glancing down is possibly the worst thing I could do under the present circumstance, but I do it anyway.

I can't see shit, but the breath fanning over my neck tells me Layla's looking up, and with our close proximity, we're in danger of accidentally kissing.

Let go of her.

Falcon.

Move back.

Fuck.

Mint. *Did she just brush her teeth?*

Softness. *Fuck my life.* Knowing the heat I'm feeling through our clothes is coming from her body wakes up a part of my body, which should not be woken right now.

A mixture of flowers and something fresh fills my nostrils.

"Falcon?" she whispers. The darkness makes my name sound intimate on her lips.

"Yeah?" *And I sound hoarse as fuck.*

"I think they're gone now."

"Yeah."

"So… ah… you can move now."

"Yeah?"

It feels like a spell's been woven around me as my eyes adjust to the dark, and I can make out her face.

A little more than an inch away from mine.

My eyes find hers, and I know she can see me because she doesn't look away, but instead, her heartbeat speeds up, pounding against my chest as if it's trying to get to mine.

All the reasons why this would be a bad idea fade to nothing, leaving only one thought – I want to kiss this girl more than anything.

Chapter 5

Layla

As he leans into me, my senses are overwhelmed with the way his breath fans over my forehead, and his body presses against mine. He makes my heart pound out of control.

Crap, I can't fall for him.

I've barely warned myself when his breath keeps moving down until it wafts over my lips, making them tingle to life.

Common sense whispers for me to step back, but my body refuses to listen.

I can feel the hard muscle of Falcon's chest as it presses against mine, and it makes me feel small. Not in a bad way but more in a feminine way.

What the hell am I thinking? This is Falcon Reyes we're talking about.

His eyes find mine in the dark, and it only makes my heart beat faster.

Please don't let him feel it. Please. Ugh, he's going to know I feel attra-

My thoughts come to a screeching halt as Falcon slowly begins to close the already small distance between us.

Is he going to kiss me?

Does he even like me?

I'm pretty sure he despises me.

Right?

Maybe he does like me a little?

Suddenly the door opens behind Falcon, and light spills into the closet. My eyes widen when I see just how close we are, and instead of pulling away, Falcon's eyes stay locked with mine.

"Mr. Reyes?" The voice has us pulling apart. I step back and bumping into the stupid bucket again, I lose my footing and fall backward, only to bump into a set of racks.

Falcon grabs hold of my arm and yanks me forward as he moves out of the tiny space. He doesn't even bother acknowledging the poor janitor who looks shocked at finding us in his maintenance closet.

"I'm sorry," I call to the man before paying attention to keeping up with Falcon, who has a tight grip on my hand, so I don't face-plant at his feet.

We're halfway across the lawn when I notice the other students staring at us.

"Falcon, people are looking at us," I hiss while yanking back against his hold. My words make him stop, and when he slackens his grip on me, I manage to tug my arm free.

When I see the intense look in Falcon's eyes, I quickly look away, not ready to face what almost happened between us.

"I have to go." With a half-hearted wave, I rush away from him, so he doesn't have time to say something I may not be ready to hear.

After being stuck in the maintenance closet with Falcon, I've had a slight heart attack every time my phone beeped.

I was caught off guard by the attraction I felt, and it's only made me feel awkward around Falcon. Letting out a sigh, I pick up my phone, and when I see Falcon's name on the screen, my heart immediately sets off at a crazy pace.

A miserable whining sound escapes my lips as I tap on the message.

'There's a messenger in the lobby with a document for me. Sign for it and bring it up to my suite.'

"You have got to be joking." Sulking, I get up and walk out of my room. When I see the messenger, I ask, "You have a parcel for Falcon Reyes?"

The man glances at me, then down at the envelope. "Yes."

"I'll sign for it."

When I'm done, I watch the guy leave then huffily walk toward the elevators.

"Just get it over with. You have to face him at some point." The doors open with a ping, and I step inside.

By the time I step out on the top floor, I've made the decision to leave the envelope in front of his door and to make a run for it.

I'm fresh out of luck because before I reach Falcon's suite, the door opens. I only realize I'm holding my breath when Lake steps out into the passage.

"Lake!" Darting forward, I shove the envelope into his hands. "Give it to Falcon. Thanks!"

I turn to make a quick escape, but Lake grabs hold of my shoulder. "Hold up. He's just going to sign it, then you have to deliver it."

"Deliver it?" I repeat, not liking the sound of that at all. Wearing a pair of shorts and a t-shirt, I'm not dressed to deliver anything.

Lake pushes the envelope back into my hands, then gives me a smile before he leaves me standing in front of the open door.

"I don't have all day, Layla," I hear Falcon call from inside, and I resist the urge to push out my bottom lip because I really feel sorry for myself right now.

Sucking it up, I step inside the suite and then blink at all the luxury. Damn, his room makes mine look like the maid's quarters.

I feel grossly underdressed as I slowly walk to where Falcon is sitting on a couch.

"I'm signing the damn thing now. If it's so urgent, you should've brought it over yourself," he snaps, and it's only then I see that he's on the phone.

With a dark glare, Falcon holds his hand out to me. I begin to put the envelope in his hand when he pulls back and pinching the bridge of his nose, growls, "Open the damn envelope and hand me the document."

Normally I'd tell him to go to hell, but I've never seen him so cold and angry and decide to play it safe. Biting my tongue, I remove the sheet of paper from the envelope and give it to him.

While he reads it, I take the opportunity to look out the huge windows at the gorgeous view outside.

"Julian." Falcon's voice is filled with ice, and it makes a shiver race down my spine. "Over my dead body will I sign this."

I slowly begin to inch toward the door, not sure I should be overhearing this conversation.

I don't know what Julian says, but Falcon darts up off the couch. "Well, then you will just have to get used to seeing me at future board meetings because hell will freeze over before I give you power of attorney over my shares." Letting out an angry growl, he throws his phone in my direction. The thing flies by me like a heat-seeking missile before it crashes against the wall.

Having the crap scared out of me, I stare at Falcon before I finally manage to look to where the pieces of the phone lie on the floor.

Falcon takes a couple of deep breaths, and as he looks at me, realization washes over his face. "Shit, I'm sorry, Layla."

There's a time and place for everything, and my gut tells me now is not the time to start a fight with Falcon. He apologized, and it's clear he's stressed out.

"I'm going to go if you don't need anything else," I say, my voice tight from all the tension in the room. I take a step closer to the door, and for a moment it looks like Falcon wants to say something else, but instead, he just nods.

Rushing out of the room, I place my hand over my thumping heart. "Holy crap, that was intense! I wonder what it was about," I whisper as I step into the elevator.

It's been two days since the almost kiss, and a day since I was almost hit by Falcon's phone, and I have to admit, I'm feeling stressed out by it all.

It doesn't take much effort to avoid Falcon, and I think the reason for it is because he's avoiding me as well. For some weird reason the thought of Falcon avoiding me sucks.

Feeling uneasy because of everything that's happened the past couple of days, I decide to put on my sneakers and go for a jog. It always helps me find my balance again.

Dressed in my running gear, I head towards the trail, which starts behind the restaurant on campus. I haven't had much time to explore yet, and as my feet steadily thump over a wooden bridge, a smile begins to form around my lips. All the trees and bushes bathe the trail in a deep green, which makes the air feel fresher.

I make my way up the trail until I reach a look-out point with a breathtaking view of the surrounding landscape. Taking a moment to stretch, I drink in the sight before me.

This is what I needed. I'm going to make this a part of my daily routine from now on.

Being mesmerized by nature, I think back to the conversation I overheard yesterday. Falcon must be under a lot of pressure. Until I saw that side to him, I always thought he was just another one of the spoiled students, but board meetings? Power of attorney?

I'm pretty sure Julian is his older brother. Mom mentioned the name before. It didn't sound like there was any love between them.

Sadness creeps into my heart for Falcon.

What kind of life does he really live?

Coming to this school, all I saw was the wealth the other students were born into.

Yeah, you might have judged them all a little too harshly.

Might have? A little?

I shake my head lightly, disappointed in myself.

Dad always said money is the root of all evil, and it's only now that I'm beginning to understand the true meaning of those words. These students don't have the freedom I have. They have to act a certain way that's acceptable to the standards of their wealth bracket.

It's really sad. What's the use of having so much money if you can't enjoy life? Letting out a sigh, I make a resolution to judge less and to understand more.

Checking my watch, I notice I've been out here for almost an hour. I stretch one more time to warm my muscles again and begin the jog back toward the campus.

As I'm coming around a bend, I spot Grayson standing to the left and move to the right side of the trail so I can jog by him. The peaceful moment I just had is tainted by an irritating feeling I always have when I see the guy. Besides him coming onto me every damn chance he gets, annoying the ever-loving shit out of me, I can't say there's anything I like about him.

"Hey," he says as I'm about to pass by him.

"Hey," I mumble back, keeping my eyes on the path ahead. The last thing I want to do is give him a reason to strike up a conversation with me.

To my dismay, he falls into step next to me. "Not every day I get you alone."

I ignore his words, doing my best to not let my irritation show on my face.

Reaching out, he takes hold of my forearm, and I have no choice but to stop when he pulls me to a halt. "You know, for a freshman, you have a lot of attitude."

I clench my jaw, so I don't retort with, *'For a senior, you think you're entitled to a lot of liberties.'* Instead, I pull my arm free and say, "I have assignments waiting, so you'll have to excuse me."

I take a step forward but stop when Grayson moves to block my way.

My patience begins to evaporate and my annoyance spikes. "I really don't have time for this, so I'm just going to be blunt. I'm not interested in you in any way."

When I try to get around him, he matches my step to the left, blocking me again. "I didn't ask whether you were interested in me." The hurt tone of his voice contradicts his words.

He takes a step forward, closing some of the distance between us, but I take one backward, which makes a frown settle on his forehead. "I go hunting with my father," he randomly states, and it takes me a moment to understand what he's saying. "You want to know what's the most exciting part?"

"I'm not interested," I repeat my words from earlier.

"The hunt," he continues. The corners of his mouth turn down in a haughty sneer, and it makes the tiny hairs on the back of my neck stand up. "There's nothing like the thrill of a chase, and you making me chase after you only reminds me of it."

"I'm not making you do anything. Seriously, I'm not playing hard to get. I. Am. Not. Interested. In. You," I enunciate the words. Damn, I've never met someone with such thick skin before.

His hand shoots up between us, and wrapping his fingers around the back of my neck, he yanks me closer.

Cheese. He had cheese for lunch.

The smell of his breath makes my stomach turn.

"Impossible," he whispers, and when the blue of his eyes darken to midnight, I feel a sensation of apprehension slither down my spine. "Girls like you never say no to someone like me."

"Girls like me?" offended, I spit the words out.

"You all want a taste of a man who's way above your shitty little lives."

Holy crap, this guy is conceited and egotistical to the point where he's ludicrous.

He begins to lean in as if he's going to kiss me, which has my self-defense instincts roaring to life. Bringing my hands up between us, I push against his chest while moving to the side so I can pull my neck free from his hold. He only budges a couple of inches, but then I feel his muscles tense under my palms, and tightening his grip on the back of my neck, he pulls me toward him until his mouth smacks hard against mine.

There's a moment in every situation where you realize your mistake – I shouldn't have even talked to this guy because he's the type who twists your words into what he wants to hear and believe.

Knowing things are about to get seriously out of hand, and I can't have that happening alone out here in the woods with this creep, I shove as hard as I can while twisting my body away from his.

I manage to free myself from his hold and try to dart away, but he grabs hold of my t-shirt, and in the process of yanking me back to him, I hear my sleeve rip.

The bastard!

"What's your damn problem?" I snap at him. His grip on my arm is so tight, I only end up hurting myself when I try to wrench it free. "You're hurting me, Grayson. Let go."

Tilting his head to the right, his eyes narrow on me. "Do you think you're in a position to tell me what to do? It must be true," he tsks, shaking his head.

"What?" I almost growl the word because I'm seriously losing my temper with this jerk.

"That blondes are dumb." The sneer on his face deepens, only making him look more arrogant.

As if that's possible.

Having had enough of this creep, I try to pry his fingers away from my arm with my right hand, and when it doesn't work, only making him chuckle, I dig my nails into his skin.

"Fuck," he snaps, but at least his fingers spring loose, and I use the moment to put as much distance between us as I can. Sprinting down the trail, I'm only aware of the fact that I have to get back to the campus, not having any time to think about my emotions or what just happened.

I'm so freaking focused on running as fast as I can that I let out a scream when Grayson plows into me from behind.

Shit, he's faster than me.

Wrapping his arms around me from behind, he drags me off the trail. Being pulled backward, it feels as if the woods are swallowing me whole as the trees close in around me.

Oh, God. This is bad. Really bad.

I start to struggle in his hold, doing my best to throw my body forward to where the trail is. I can't let him drag me into the woods. God only knows what will happen then.

While struggling, I accidentally slam the back of my head against his chin, but it works because his arms slacken their hold on me, and I manage to dart forward.

My breaths explode over my dry lips, burning down my throat while my heart is pounding like crazy in my chest.

Run, Layla!

My panicked inner-voice spurs me on as I rush over the unsteady ground while dodging trees.

Roots slow me down, and feeling frantic and distressed, a cry escapes me when Grayson grabs hold of my ponytail.

"You're asking for trouble," he growls while hauling me back.

I lose my footing and crash into the hard ground. Within seconds, Grayson is on top of me, making fear explode through my body. Pinning me down with his weight, he grabs hold of my t-shirt and rips it in the front, exposing my sports bra. His mouth comes brutally down on mine, and not thinking twice, I sink my teeth into his bottom lip. I get the desired reaction as he pulls away with a howl of pain.

Brushing his thumb over the broken skin, he glares down at the blood on his finger. "Bitch, you actually bit me?"

"You're sick," I scream angrily as I crawl away from him. I climb to my feet when he grips hold of my shoulder. Fear and anger swirl inside of me, creating a dizzying storm of emotions. He raises his hand, and before I realize what's happening, the clammy skin of his palm connects with my cheek.

I hear the slap, but it takes a stunned moment before I feel the sting spread over the side of my face.

It's a stunned moment that gives Grayson the chance to grab hold of the front of my torn t-shirt while raising his hand again.

But my shock is quickly shoved aside by a rage I've never felt before.

He slapped me.

Seeing red, I bring my knee up between us. When it connects with his groin, I feel some of the vulnerability he made me endure give way to courage and determination to save myself.

Bending over with his hands cupping his groin, he lets out a pain-filled groan.

"Don't ever touch me again," I hiss enraged before turning around and quickly making my way back to the trail.

As I reach the trail, I hear his footsteps crunching right behind me, and it only spurs me on to push harder. Just before the bridge, leading to the back of the restaurant on campus, I hear Grayson roar, "You're going to pay for that!"

His hand smacks the back of my head, and as I lose my footing, he shoves me forward, making me fall onto my knees. The impact shudders through my body, and it burns where the skin has been scraped off my kneecaps.

Before I can manage to get up, Grayson grabs hold of my ponytail and yanking me to the side, his fist connects with my jaw, right beneath my ear. A buzzing sound fills my hearing, and a sharp pain shoots through my head.

Dazed, a desperate feeling bleeds into my soul.

Get up and run away.

The words lend strength to my legs and pushing myself up, I blindly lash out, scratching every surface of exposed skin I can find. I somehow manage to head butt Grayson again, and the impact only dazes me more, but I refuse to give in to the frenzied terror whirling in my chest.

As I repeatedly lunge forward, hitting and clawing at Grayson, I feel animalistic. I feel the need to inflict as much pain on him, as he has inflicted on me. I want him to feel the same fear and vulnerability he made me feel by trying to use his strength as a man against me.

I never thought I'd be this kind of person.

I used to be the kind of girl who runs to jump on her bed after switching off the light.

I used to be the kind of girl who runs from a wasp while screeching, *'you win… you win.'*

Feeling absolutely sickened by what's happening, I shove Grayson roughly away, then set off running. I push myself forward and only feel a sliver of the brutal tension ease when I near the dorms.

"Layla!" Kingsley's panicked voice penetrates through the shock, fear, and maddening rage I'm engulfed in, and it acts like a switch, instantly draining me of all my strength.

My legs feel wobbly as I slow down, and when I come to a stop, I reach out and grab hold of Kingsley's shoulders so I won't crumble to the ground. Tears burn the back of my eyes, and I begin to shiver as if I'm freezing.

"What the hell happened?" she asks, the blood draining from her always rosy cheeks.

I open my mouth, but instead of words, only a sob comes out. Kingsley pulls me against her, and when her arms fold tightly around me, I let the tears fall. After the horrific encounter with Grayson, I finally feel some sense of safety in her arms.

"I'm going to fucking sue you! Look what you've done to my face." Grayson's roar behind me brings the panic and fear flooding back through my veins.

Letting go of Kingsley, I glance over my shoulder as I dart to my left and into The Hope Diamond so I can get to the safety of my room, but end up slamming into someone else.

"Layla?" Lake's voice sounds distant.

It must be the distress making me dizzy. I don't think I can fight for much longer.

The thought makes a helpless feeling swamp my heart.

Somehow, I manage to focus on the face in front of me. I see the soft brown eyes, and they're in total contrast to the blue ones, which will be haunting my nightmares from now on.

I grab hold of Lake's shirt and force the words past the lump of fear in my throat, "Help me."

Feeling drained of all my strength, I need someone stronger than me, and I'm hoping to God Lake will be that someone.

Lake brings his hands to my face, and cupping my cheeks, he leans down to look at me. Worry fills his eyes as he takes in my haggard state.

"What happened?" I see the words forming on his lips, but I can't hear them past the rushing in my ears as the shock from the ordeal begins to set in.

Staying close to Lake, I turn so I can point a trembling finger to outside. When I see Kingsley screaming at Grayson, guilt ripples through me.

I just left her out there with him.

Lake pulls away from me, and it draws a whimpering sob from my burning chest. The trembling in my body increases uncontrollably as my eyes stay glued to Lake, where he's jogging to Kingsley's side.

When Lake's fist makes Grayson's head snap back, my vision begins to blur. Exhausted to my core, the last of my strength fades from my legs.

As darkness creeps in, arms come from behind and wrapping around me, they keep me from going down like a ton of bricks.

Chapter 6

Falcon

"Have you heard from Julian again?" Mason asks while we're going down in the elevator.

The doors slide open as I answer, "No. I still can't believe he thought I'd give him power of attorney over my shares."

"Yeah, that was a bold move."

Stepping into the foyer, I see Lake talking to someone. "He's going to be late for dinner with his parents," I mention. Lake left the suite ten minutes before us for his usual Wednesday dinner appointment. I'm surprised to still find him here because he never keeps his parents waiting. Lake darts forward and breaks out into a jog.

Yeah, get your ass to the restaurant.

The thought freezes in my mind when my eyes land on Layla's tearstained face. Her body shudders with every sob leaving her.

What the fuck?

Her hair's a mess, and her white and blue shirt's ripped in the front. It takes a moment for me to process what I'm seeing.

Red bruises on her way too pale face.

Wide eyes, unfocused and wild with panic.

Leaves in her hair.

Scrapes all over her legs.

My eyes travel down her body, and with each bruise and blood splatter I take in, merciless anger grows inside of me.

Somehow, I manage to move forward so I can get to her. Unsteadily, she turns away from me, and I reach her just in time as her legs give way. Wrapping my arms around her from behind, I hold her to me so she doesn't fall to the ground.

My eyes meet Mason's before we both look to where Lake is hitting Grayson.

"I have her. Go help Lake." The words sound weird as if it's not my voice leaving my lips.

As Mason rushes toward the doors, I loosen my hold a little, so I can move around Layla. Tilting my head to the side, I try to get a better look at her, but her hair's a mess and hiding the left side of her face.

"What happened?" I ask, and bringing a hand up to brush her hair out of the way, I freeze when she flinches.

The severity of the moment hits me right in the gut, making it feel like my breaths are getting stuck in my throat. I've lived a sheltered life and never had to deal with something like this before. I have no fucking idea how to handle this situation. Emotions begin to intensify deep within my heart, ranging from protectiveness to worry.

I struggle to stay calm, and I'm just about to ask again when her eyes focus on my face. She hiccups past the sobs, "Falcon."

Moving slower this time, I bring a hand up and gently tuck the wild strands behind her ear. Seeing the other bruise on her jaw makes my anger spike rapidly.

Assuming Grayson has something to do with this, I ask, "Did Grayson –" The rage makes me sound angry as fuck, and not wanting to frighten Layla more, I clear my throat before whispering, "Did Grayson do this to you?"

She begins to nod, but before she can answer me, a commotion behind us scares the shit out her. Grabbing hold of my jacket, she steps right into me, hiding behind the little protection the fabric offers. Her reaction makes my protective side explode to life like never before. A door slams closed behind us, making Layla startle again. I wrap my left arm around her shoulders, and place my right behind her head, wanting her to feel some sort of safety in my arms.

I glance back to see what the hell is happening. Mason shoves Grayson forward, making him fall to his knees on the marble floor. Grayson quickly climbs to his feet and moves away from Mason while struggling to pull his phone from his pocket. "I'm pressing charges against you," he dares to threaten Mason.

I'm used to seeing Mason out of control, but when Lake walks right up to Grayson, getting in his face, surprise ripples through me.

"You want to press charges? You're not the fucking victim here!"

Grayson uses his palm to wipe some of the blood away from the cut above his left eye. "She fucking bit me!" he roars, the veins bulging in his neck. Pointing at his face with a shaking finger, he continues to rant, "Look at the scratches! If it scars, she's paying the fucking bill."

"What did you do to make her bite and scratch you?" Kingsley yells, her cheeks stained red, and her hands trembling. I've never seen Kingsley so upset before.

"I did nothing. The bitch is crazy. This is what happens when you allow low-lives into Trinity."

Glancing back at Layla, something in me shifts when she cowers closer to me.

I bring my hands to her shoulders and try to pull her a little back. "Layla, tell me what happened."

She shakes her head and burrows her way back against my chest. Without turning around to look at Grayson because I know I will lose my shit and beat him to death, I growl, "Restrain him in the suite. I'll deal with him once I've taken care of Layla."

Needing to put some distance between us and Grayson, I bend down and placing an arm beneath her legs, and another behind her back, I lift her up. "Kingsley, get Layla's door for me."

Kingsley darts around me to retrieve the keycard from Layla's pocket. She has to swipe it twice before she manages to open the door. I step inside and head to the couch. Placing Layla down on it, I glance to Kingsley, where she's closing the door. "Call for a doctor."

The word doctor gets Layla's attention because she begins to shake her head. "No doctor. I'm not hurt."

Crouching in front of her, I almost place a hand on her bruised knee, but stop just in time. Needing to touch her in some way, I let my arm rest on the couch beside her leg. "You're not hurt?" I ask incredulously. "Layla, you need

91

medical attention. Either the doctor comes here, or I'm taking you to hospital."

Her eyes dart to mine. "No hospital. My mom can't know."

"We can talk about that later," I say to pacify her and give her hip a gentle squeeze.

"Make the call, Kingsley," I order while pulling my own phone from my pocket. I bring up Lake's number and wait until I hear him pick up.

"Make sure Mason doesn't kill the fucker," I say.

"That seriously hurts my feelings," Mason replies, making me frown.

"Where's Lake?"

"Beating the shit out of Grayson."

"Fuck, Mason, separate them," I snap. "Call Lake's father. We need legal here to handle this fucking mess."

"I'm calling him now, so he doesn't have to deal with a murder case."

I can't blame the guys. If I had to see Grayson now, I'd be facing murder charges soon.

After calling the doctor, Kingsley comes to sit next to Layla, and I hate moving away from her, but Kingsley will know better how to handle the situation.

I take a seat on the opposite side of the coffee table. Kingsley wraps her arms around Layla while my eyes jump from one bruise to the next.

What happened between her and Grayson?

Dark thoughts begin to force their way into my mind, making me grind my teeth. I know what type of person he is, which only makes the images in my mind spin out of control.

"Layla. Did Gray —" My voice sounds hoarse from the dread spinning a web around my heart. Not being able to say the exact words I'm thinking, I try to be sensitive about my approach. "Did he force himself on you?"

My question has shock rippling through the room. Kingsley pulls back, her eyes wide with horror as they jump all over Layla's face.

Layla's movements are jerky as she brings her hands to her chest, and taking hold of the torn t-shirt, she tries to cover herself.

The last time I felt this kind of emotion was at Jennifer's funeral. Seeing Mason's grief for the loss of his sister had my heart breaking for my friend.

With the torturous scenarios flooding my mind, and Layla's traumatized state, the urge to punch something is overwhelming.

Getting up, I walk around the table and crouch in front of Layla again. I place my hands on either side of her and try to catch her eyes as I ask, "Did he?"

Her eyes dance wildly over my face, and she shakes her head. "No." She grips the pieces of her shirt tighter.

I feel zero relief after hearing her say no, and it makes me agitated. Glancing to Kingsley, I ask, "What's taking the doctor so long?"

"I'll call him again." Kingsley darts up and races to the door. When she steps out into the foyer, I take the spot she vacated. I'm careful as I place my arm around Layla's shoulders, and when she turns to me and rests her forehead to my shoulder, I feel a slither of relief.

After the doctor treats Layla, he gives her something to help calm her down.

Just as there's a knock on the door, she asks the doctor, "Can I shower?"

Opening the door, my eyes land on Mr. Cutler, and for the first time tonight, I feel the tension ease a little.

As Mr. Cutler steps into the room, the doctor answers, "Yes, you can bathe or shower. I'll leave the ointment with you. Reapply it when you're done."

When Kingsley begins to help Layla up from the couch, Mr. Cutler quickly mentions, "Before you shower, we need to take photos."

Layla's eyes dart from me to Mr. Cutler, which prompts me to introduce them. "This is Mr. Cutler. He's Lake's father."

The meager color Layla managed to regain drains from her face. Looking very uncomfortable, she wraps the blanket Kingsley brought her earlier tighter around her body. "I'm sorry, Mr. Cutler. They shouldn't have called you."

"Nonsense, Miss Shepard." He walks to her and taking hold of her chin, he looks at the bruises on her face. "I always knew the Stateman boy was trouble." Glancing at me from over his shoulder, he asks, "Didn't I warn you not to let him attend Trinity?"

"Yes, Sir."

Picking up his bag, the doctor says, "I'll be going now."

"Thank you for making the emergency call," I mention as I let him out before closing the door behind him.

"I understand you've had quite the traumatic evening, but I need to take photos, Miss Shepard. If this ever goes to trial, we need all the evidence we can get our hands on."

"Trial?" Layla's eyes begin to shine with tears, and I quickly rush to her side.

"There won't be a trial. I promise."

"But photos?" She shakes her head, looking utterly drained of her fight for life. "I don't want proof out there of what happened today."

"Miss Shepard, no one will see the photos unless we go to court."

A tear trickles down her cheek, and lifting my hand, I wipe it away with my thumb. Layla's eyes find mine, and the pleading look she gives me almost breaks my heart.

"I don't want my mom to know. If this gets out, I'm scared..." she swallows hard on the emotion before she continues, "This might jeopardize her career. It will drag CRC into the mess, and I can't have that. It will be a media frenzy."

Bringing my hands to her face, I cup her cheeks and keep my eyes locked with her. "It will never get out."

"But Grayson —" she begins to argue, but I cut her off.

"Don't worry about Grayson. I'll take care of him. I know it's hard right now but try to trust me."

After a couple of seconds, she wets her lips, then says, "I'll only consent to photos if they're taken with my phone, and I keep them. I'm sorry, I need to know no one else has access to them."

I look at Mr. Cutler to see what he thinks, but instead of arguing with Layla, he adds, "Gather every leaf and place it in a bag with everything you're wearing right now."

"Okay," Layla answers quickly, relief softening the lines on her forehead.

Taking a deep breath, Mr. Cutler begins to walk toward the door. "Let's go deal with Mr. Stateman." He suddenly stops and looks back at Layla. "Unfortunately, life is filled with degenerates like Grayson. I apologize that this happened to you at Trinity Academy."

I give Layla's shoulder a squeeze then pick up the keycard from the coffee table. "I'm taking the card. I'll be back as soon as the problem is taken care of."

"Thank you." The words are soft, but the grateful look on Layla's face makes every unpleasant moment worth it.

Walking into the suite I share with Mason and Lake, my eyes burn a hole through Grayson, where he's sitting on the couch. When he sees Mr. Cutler, he quickly gets up.

"Mr. Stateman," Mr. Cutler says, his voice thick with disapproval. He walks over to the dining table and places his briefcase on it then opens it. "Come, take a seat."

While Grayson does as he's instructed, Mr. Cutler looks at Lake. "Are you alright, my boy?"

Lake looks down at the blood splatters on his hands and shoving them behind his back, he nods. "Thank you for coming, Dad."

Mr. Cutler glances at Mason.

"For a change, I'm the good one," Mason jokes,

which has me shaking my head. Trust Mason to say something like that at a time like this.

"Hell will freeze over, and I was hoping to retire in a warm place, so let's not horse around about you being good," Mr. Cutler jokes back, and it helps to ease the tension in the room.

Clearing his throat, Grayson brings the attention back to himself. "Mr. Cutler, I know this looks bad, but I'd appreciate it if you could hear my side of the story."

Mr. Cutler takes a document from his briefcase and sets it down in front of Grayson. "Mr. Stateman, if you wish to

98

have legal representation present, then I recommend you call them now."

"Legal representation?" Grayson asks, and his eyes dart down to the document. "Non-disclosure agreement?"

I go to stand next to Mr. Cutler, so the table's between Grayson and me because it's hard talking to the bastard and not being able to kill him.

"After signing the NDA, you will leave the campus immediately and never set foot here again." It's the only option I'm giving him.

Grayson shoots up out of the chair but flinches in pain as he grabs his side. "Why should I be the one to leave?"

"If you don't, I'll leak your dirty little secret to every media house in this country," I threaten. The footage I have of Grayson doing drugs with an underaged girl will be enough to damage his family name, if not ruin it.

"No one is going to bother to hear my side of the story? You're all just going to believe whatever she said?"

The offended look on Grayson's face has me grinding my teeth as I lean forward. Placing my hands on the table, I don't hide my hatred for the bastard. "This isn't a hearing, and I'm not a judge. I don't care about your side. Sign the form and get off our property before I lose the little patience I have left."

"Wow." Giving me a dark glare, Grayson holds his hand out. "Give me a pen."

Mr. Cutler takes a pen from the inside pocket of his jacket, and as he places it on Grayson's palm, he says, "I'm not sure what the boys have on you, but like Falcon stated; this isn't a hearing. Be forewarned, Mr. Stateman. One wrong move on your part, and we'll have our next meeting in court."

Grayson at least has the decency to look chastised, but then he knows he doesn't stand a chance against us. He signs the document before dropping the pen on it.

"If I leave, I want the video," he dares to demand of me.

"You're in no position to make demands," I cut him off. Picking up the document, I hand it to Mr. Cutler. "Thank you so much for coming. Let me walk you out."

"My boy, give your mom a call. She'll only stop worrying once she hears from you," Mr. Cutler says to Lake as he closes his briefcase.

"I'll call her right now," Lake answers, and he begins to reach for his phone where it's lying on the coffee table.

"Wash your hands first," Mr. Cutler orders while shaking his head.

"Ah… yes." Lake rushes to the restroom.

Mason takes a step closer to Grayson. "Do I get the honor of escorting him off the property?"

"Dear, God," Mr. Cutler sighs. "It pains me knowing our future is in your hands, Mason. I can only imagine what the board meetings will be like. Walk me out and let Falcon take care of the problem."

Mason jogs over to Mr. Cutler's side and throws an arm around his shoulders. "Admit it, you can't wait for me to join the board meetings. I'll liven the place up."

"Like a dynamite stick in a chicken coop."

I wait for them to leave the suite, then turn to Grayson. "You have ten minutes."

"Or what? I'll take my fucking time," he sneers. "I meant what I said. I want that video."

I close my eyes for a moment, trying my God's-honest-best to not lose my shit. "Fuck this," I growl, and stalking toward him, I pull my arm back. The relief I've been looking for rushes through me as my fist connects with his skin. "You will get off my property before I kill you. The video should really be the least of your worries."

With the arrogant smirk wiped off his face, Grayson begins to look panicked, which is about fucking time. "You're not fucking untouchable, Falcon," he yells.

With the whole of CRC Holdings standing behind me, I slowly begin to smile. "Yes, I am."

The confidence in my voice rattles Grayson even more, and he begins to stutter, "F-fine… T-this place is h-highly overrated anyway and not t-the only Academy I can attend."

I follow Grayson out of the building and watch him get into his car. When he drives off, I call security at the front gate to update them to never allow entrance to Grayson Stateman again. Ending the call, I stand in the parking area beside the dormitories and glance from one building to the other until my eyes stop on The Hope Diamond.

Whoever said money can buy you status was grossly mistaken.

Chapter 7

Layla

Kingsley fell asleep a couple of minutes ago, and the silence has started to gnaw on my frail nerves. I glance down at her peaceful face where she's out cold on the bed. I might not have known her for long, but today she proved her friendship to me in a way no one should have to.

"Thank you," I whisper, unbelievably grateful for everything she did for me today.

I walk to the window in my bedroom and stare at the dark night outside. I feel edgy, as if I'm being caged in by the walls of my room, but I'm too scared to go outside.

This morning I felt safe as I walked around campus. It never crossed my mind to be on guard. And now...

My eyes follow the path down below until it fades into the night.

Now I'm not sure I'll ever feel safe again.

I know I shouldn't let the incident taint my entire life, but it's hard to not let it. Falcon said he'd deal with Grayson, but how can I stay on the same campus as that guy? How many of the students are like Grayson, and I foolishly trusted them with my safety?

Trust. It's such a fragile thing. One blow is enough to obliterate it.

I hear the door to my suite opening, and for a second, my body stiffens, and my heart begins to beat faster. Only when Lake walks into my room do I let out the breath I was holding.

My eyes meet Lake's, and the warmth I see in them chase some of the chill from my body. He walks to where I am and without saying anything, wraps his arms around me.

There's no urge to pull away. Not when it comes to Lake.

"Thank you for helping me," I whisper against his shoulder. Closing my eyes, I focus on the fact that I feel safe with him. I remind myself not all men are like Grayson.

Lake is safe.

He presses a kiss to the side of my head, then asks, "Do you need anything?"

I shake my head, and when he begins to pull back my hands shoot up to his sides, and I grab hold of his shirt. "Just one more minute."

His arms tighten around me again, and it's so comforting, I struggle not to cry from the relief it brings.

"How does Kingsley manage to sleep after tonight?" I hear Mason ask. Lifting my head, I peek over Lake's shoulder and see both Falcon and Mason staring at Kingsley, who's lying haphazardly across the bed.

This time when Lake pulls away, I let go of him, even though I'd be happy to hug him right through the night.

"Thank you," I say again. I don't think I'll ever be able to say that enough to him.

He lifts a hand to the left side of my face, and a sad look crosses his features as he brushes his thumb over the bruise on my jaw. "You're welcome."

With his hand being so close to my face, a glimpse of red catches my eye. Reaching up, I take hold of Lake's hand so I can see it better. There are bruises on his knuckles, and the sight of them upsets me all over again.

"You got hurt? I'm sorry."

"You should see what –" Mason stops mid-sentence when Falcon slaps him against the arm.

"She doesn't need to know," he whispers, giving Mason a look of warning.

"Let me put some of the ointment the doctor left on your hand." I pull Lake to the foot of my bed and nod towards it. "Sit down." I try to force a smile as I walk by Falcon and Mason, but immediately feel self-conscious of the marks on my face. Grabbing the ointment, I keep my eyes on it while walking back to Lake. I kneel down on the floor and welcome the distraction of tending to his cuts.

When I'm done, and desperately need something else to do, I offer, "Can I make you all coffee?"

"No, thanks," Mason answers first. "I'm going to head up to the suite. I just wanted to check on you."

"Thanks for everything you guys did for me tonight. I really appreciate it."

"Always a pleasure, babe," Mason says, then walks out of the room. I stare after him for a moment, thinking he's not such a bad guy after all.

"Call if you need anything," Lake says, and giving my elbow a squeeze, he presses another kiss to my temple. When he leaves, I have no choice but to look at Falcon.

Lake feels like an older brother, and it makes it easy being around him.

Mason's aloof attitude and quick temper keeps everyone at a distance, including me.

But Falcon... Confused doesn't begin to describe how I feel. Before the crap hit the fan, my biggest worry was the attraction I felt for him. Tonight, he took control and dealt with my problem.

While it was happening, I didn't have time to process anything, but as our eyes meet and I see the remaining embers of worry still smoldering in them, I know it's too late from keeping him out of my heart.

"You need to get some sleep as well," he says, then gestures to the bed. "Which side do you usually sleep on?"

"The left."

Placing a knee on the bed, Falcon slips his arms under Kingsley and moves her to the right side. "Hopefully she stays like this, otherwise just kick her off," he comments while covering her with a blanket.

"Never thought I'd see the day where you tuck someone into bed," I tease.

Falcon's eyes find mine, and then the corner of his mouth lifts into a sexy grin. "Don't tell anyone. It would ruin my reputation."

"Your secret is safe with me."

Falcon walks to where I'm still awkwardly standing in front of the bed, and placing a hand on my lower back, he gives me a gentle nudge. "Get in bed. This will be your only chance to have me tuck you in."

I let out a breath of laughter. "You don't have to. You must be tired as well. I'll let you out first."

He shakes his head and nudges me again. "I know I don't have to. Get in bed."

Knowing Falcon won't stop until I listen to him, I walk to the left side and crawl under the covers. He walks out of the room, and I wonder if he's leaving, but then he comes back with the chair from my work desk. He sets it down next to the bed then takes a seat.

"You really don't have to stay." *Because there's no way I'll sleep knowing you're here.*

"I know." He leans back and stretches his legs out in front of him. "Close your eyes."

Instead of listening, my eyes find his. He has so much confidence, I wish I could borrow some.

"Sleep, Layla," he whispers.

I shake my head and look down at my hands, where I'm clutching the covers.

"Are you scared?" Falcon's voice is a low murmur, and it makes me feel like I could share all my secrets with him.

108

I nod, not taking my eyes away from my hands.

"Move up," he says, and raising to his feet, he comes to sit next to me. He leans back against the headboard and crosses his arms. "I'll stay until you fall asleep."

It's clear he won't leave until I'm asleep, so I decide to fake it so he can go get some rest himself. I close my eyes and pull the blanket up until it covers the bruise on my jaw.

I hope the marks fade quickly because there's no way I can go to any of my classes looking like this.

I begin to worry about all the work I'll miss when Falcon slides down until he's lying next to me, and pushing an arm under my head, he uses his other hand to pull me against his chest. "Stop worrying. I'll take care of everything." His voice is a low murmur, and with the way he's holding me, I can almost believe he cares about me.

"Why are you so nice to me?"

"It happened on my property. I'd do this for anyone." The answer sounds well-rehearsed.

When I try to pull back so I can look up at him, he brings a hand up to the back of my head to stop me. Pressing a kiss to the top of my head, he whispers, "Shh, Layla. No more questions."

Giving in, I close my eyes and try not to think why Falcon is nice to me, or about anything that happened today.

Instead of being distressed about the incident, my last thoughts are of how calm I feel having Falcon by my side.

Falcon kept his word. When I woke, there was only Kingsley, who was lying half on top of me. She left soon after waking, and I've been cleaning my suite since.

A knock at the door has my eyes darting to it. Wondering who it could be, I walk closer. "Who is it?" I ask, which is something I haven't done before.

"It's me. Quickly, the bag is heavy."

I yank the door open and can't help but smile when I see Kingsley with a huge bag of candy, her laptop, and an overnight bag.

"We deserve a day of pigging out and pampering ourselves. I think I managed to bring everything."

"It looks like you're moving in," I tease while closing the door. I follow her to the couch and watch as she dumps the bag of candy over the coffee table. "And you raided the candy aisle."

"This is my private stash." She opens her overnight bag and pulls out one facial product after the other from it. "I swear it feels like I aged ten years after yesterday."

"You and me both," I agree as I sit down next to her.

"No, get up. We need to wash our hands and faces first before we start."

"But … I just showered."

Giving me a stern look, she points to the restroom. "We need to do a proper cleanse."

Kingsley's definition of a proper cleanse means scrubbing off a layer of skin.

"How can this be good for you?" I ask, following her back to the couch.

"We need to remove all the dead cells so all the goodness can soak in."

Sitting down, she hands me a charcoal mask. "Trust me, once we're done, you'll feel brand new."

Doing facials with Kingsley is a whole new experience, but it's nice and just the distraction I needed.

"I heard he left the Academy," she suddenly says.

"Who?" Only when the word leaves me do I realize *who*. "Really?"

"Yeah, I don't have all the details, but apparently Falcon escorted him off the campus."

"Where did you hear this?" I ask, worried that rumors are already spreading over the campus.

"I overheard two girls talking. Serena also told me Grayson called her to let her know he had to return home because of personal reasons."

"She said that? Do you believe her? You don't think he told her more? What if –"

Kingsley takes hold of my hand and gives it a squeeze. "Serena doesn't know the real reason. She wouldn't ask me if she knew. She's the type who would tell the whole world. Don't worry. I'm sure she doesn't know about what happened yesterday."

"What if he tells someone?" I voice my concern.

"I wouldn't stress about it if I were you. I'm sure Mr. Cutler took care of it all."

"It was really nice of the guys to help last night," I mention.

"Yeah, but honestly, I've never seen Lake so upset before." Kingsley opens a pack of Swedish Fish and pops one into her mouth. "The way he punched Grayson," she chews and swallows, then laughs, "Grayson's head went back like this." She tries to show me but only laughs harder. "His eyes rolled back." She lets out a snort then cracks up with laughter. "I think I just snorted a piece of Swedish Fish."

I begin to laugh because Kingsley's laughter is infectious. This girl walked right into my heart and staked her claim on it.

Chapter 8

Falcon

Walking to my next class, I slow my pace when I see Layla and Kingsley coming toward me.

Layla has managed to cover the bruises with makeup. Looking at her, it's almost hard to believe she's the same girl from three days ago. Her strength is admirable.

"Hi," Kingsley greets and stopping in front of me she pops a piece of chocolate into her mouth.

"Isn't it a little early for candy?" Even though the question is addressed to Kingsley, my eyes keep scanning over Layla's face for any signs that she might not be coping with the incident.

"It's never too early." Kingsley begins to walk around me and waves at Layla. "Meet me at the library after class."

"Sure."

A group of students coming toward us catches my eye, so I quickly take hold of Layla's arm and pull her closer to the wall.

"How are you doing?"

She smiles at me, and when it reaches her eyes, it makes a smile of my own tug at my mouth.

"I'm much better. Kingsley has been a mother hen," she answers. "Thank you for everything you guys did for me."

"You've already thanked us," I remind her.

"I know." She scrunches her nose, looking a little awkward. "I'm just really grateful."

Not knowing what else to say, I resort to how things were between us before the attack. "I had them set aside books on equities for me. While you're at the library, check them out."

"Okay."

"Just the person I'm looking for," Serena's voice sounds up behind me.

Whispering 'fuck', I close my eyes for a second.

"I'm going to head to class. I'll bring the books later," Layla says, leaving me to deal with Serena, who comes to stand in front of me.

"I have to get to class as well," I try to excuse myself.

Serena reaches a manicured hand out to me and places it on my arm. "I'll only take a minute."

I let out a chuckle. "You never take just a minute."

"Did you have anything to do with Grayson leaving?" This woman is so bad at hiding anything. I can see the suspicion written all over her face, but there's no way I'm giving her the answer she wants to hear.

"He left?" I feign ignorance.

"Come on, Falcon. We both know nothing happens at Trinity without you being aware of it."

I just stare at her, willing this conversation to come to a quick end.

"Fine, if you're not going to talk about Grayson, let's move on to the next subject."

"Dear God. You have more than one subject?" I grumble, not at all pleased.

"Is there something going on between you and Layla?"

I'm definitely not discussing Layla with her. I glance at the students walking by us. "You're wasting my time."

"There are rumors around campus, and I have to admit, I'm a little worried. Not like she's competition, but I'd hate to be made a fool of."

Annoyance bubbles up in my chest as my eyes settle hard on Serena. "Who I have a relationship with has

116

nothing to do with you, Serena. Don't you think you're giving yourself too much importance in my life?" I can't stop the sneer from forming around my mouth as I continue, "I hate to break it to you, but you're making yourself look like a damn idiot by running after me."

A calculating look settles hard on her face as she lifts her chin in a defensive way. "I don't think your mother would agree."

The threat only makes me angry, and taking a step forward, I don't care that I'm being intimidating toward a woman right now. "The difference between you and me is I don't give a shit about what my mother thinks. You and my mother can scheme all you want, but it's not going to happen. Neither of you has a say in my life." I take another step closer, and my voice drops low. "I will never feel anything for you. I will never kiss you. I will never share a bed with you. I will never give you my name. I. Will. Never. Marry. You." Lifting an eyebrow, I wait five seconds, so my words have time to sink in. "Have I made myself clear?"

The corners of her mouth begin to pull down, and she crosses her arms. "Careful, Falcon. If you fly too close to the sun, you'll end up burning your wings. You're not in a seat of power yet."

I can't stop the laughter from slipping over my lips. I'm done wasting another second tolerating this woman and begin to walk away. "Hey, at least I'll go down in a blaze of glory."

I've decided to skip class after the encounter with Serena, which only managed to ruin my day. On my way back to the suite, I run into Mason and Lake. "Where are you headed?"

"We're going for a swim," Lake answers. "You want to join us?"

"Sure, I'll grab my stuff and meet you at the pool."

After stopping by the suite, I head over to the pool house. Mason and Lake are already doing laps. Grabbing the hem of my shirt, I pull it over my head and toss it on the chairs, situated around the pool. I dive in and swim a couple of laps before I stop to catch my breath.

A group of girls has made themselves comfortable by the windows. The one excitedly waves when I glance in their direction. "Hi, Falcon."

During high school, I used to feel flattered by the attention, but like everything else in my life, it now irritates me.

Not bothering greeting her back, I swim over to the other side of the pool where Lake and Mason are leaning against the edge, looking just as annoyed as I feel by the intrusion.

When I reach them, Lake asks, "Are we leaving?"

"Might as well," I answer, and wait for Mason and Lake to get out before I grab hold of the railing so I can take the stairs out of the water.

My eyes land on Layla as Lake throws me a towel, which falls to the floor. Layla's eyes sweep over my body, and when her tongue darts out to wet her lips, a smirk forms on my face. That's definitely a look of interest.

When her eyes meet mine, and she sees that I caught her staring, she clears her throat and quickly turns her head to Lake. "Looking good, Lake."

My eyebrow lifts, and I glance between Lake and Layla. "You're welcome to look whenever you want," Lake teases.

"Yeah, let us know what times you'll be here, and we'll work it into our schedules," Kingsley jokes.

"We already have a fan club," Mason comments and then throws the damp towel at Kingsley.

She quickly slaps it away. "Oh, I didn't even see you there."

"Why are you here again?" Mason asks, taking a step toward Kingsley.

"Uhm… We were walking by and saw you through the windows. I just want to drop off the books Falcon asked for," Layla answers quickly, and stepping between Kingsley and Mason, she holds the books out to me. "Here you go."

I walk toward her, and when her eyes drop to my chest, they widen slightly before she glances away. I take the books from her and wait for her to look up. When she finally gives in, and her eyes meet mine, a blush creeps up her neck.

Did she hear the rumors? Is that why she's uncomfortable?

"I assume you heard the rumors?" I ask.

"Rumors?" Mason asks.

"I didn't hear anything," Lake mentions.

"Yeah, and you need to do something about it, Falcon," Kingsley says. "Layla is getting death glares from the so-called fan club." She rolls her eyes before they land on Mason with a glare.

"No, it's fine. They're just rumors. It's nothing to worry about." Layla smiles, and her eyes shift down to my chest before jumping back to my face as she begins to ramble, "Crap, not that I'm saying it's nothing to date you. I mean, who wouldn't want to date you." The blush reaches her cheeks, and she begins to fidget as panic flashes over her face. "Shit, that came out wrong." She points to the exit and begins to move backward. "I'm just going to go now. You have your books. We're good. Enjoy the swim." Her eyes drop to my chest again. "Or the drying off. Enjoy whatever you're going to do now." She swings around and quickly walks to the exit while shaking her head.

"Wow, she just buried herself alive there," Mason says then begins to laugh. "I'd pay to see that again."

"Mason, this is why people say you're an asshole," Kingsley comments drily.

"Got to live up to the title," he quips back at her just before she leaves to follow Layla.

"You're all going to drive me to alcohol," Lake grumbles as he starts to walk away.

I pick up the towel and wrap it around my waist, then grab my shirt and pull it over my head. "Wait up." I fall

121

into step next to Lake, then ask, "Is there something going on between you and Layla?"

Lake frowns and gives me a look which clearly asks if I've lost my mind. "Why would you think that? You remember I'm getting married next summer?"

"You're friendly with her," I say because thinking about it, I don't have much to base my suspicion on.

"I'm friendly with everyone. Also, let's not forget the rumor on campus is about you and Layla."

"True. Just thought I'd ask." I run a hand through my hair as we cross the street to get to The Hope Diamond.

Walking into the building, Lake gestures toward Layla's closed door. "The real question is whether it's a rumor or a fact?"

"What? Layla and me?" I let out a burst of laughter and press the button for the elevator. "Yeah, right."

The doors open, and we step inside. As they slide shut, Lake says, "When are you going to admit you like her?"

"I don't."

"You do."

"Lake."

"Falcon." He glances at me and sighs. "You like Layla. I've known you since diapers, and you wouldn't be bothered about a girl even if she laid dying at your feet.

The way you were with her the other night, it's clear you care about her."

The doors open just in time, and trying to ignore Lake's words, I stalk down the hallway, so I can get to the privacy of my room.

'It's clear you care about her.'

'You like Layla.'

Entering the suite, I head straight for my room. When I shut the door behind me, I stand and stare at the floor like an idiot that's just been hit by lightning.

When did things change from her being my assistant to me liking her? Sure, I felt a spark of attraction, but caring about the woman?

Do I really care about her?

"Damn, has there ever been a time I actually cared about a woman?" I try to think back but come up empty-handed.

"Don't overthink it," Lake calls from the other side of the door. "If you want my opinion, I think the two of you would make a great couple. She doesn't take your shit."

I yank the door open and glare at Lake. "I don't want your opinion." Slamming it shut again, I scowl at the wood.

She doesn't take my shit. I've never seen her back down from a fight.

"Fuck."

"Yep, told you," Lake chuckles.

Chapter 9

Layla

Walking into my legal writing class, I glance at Serena, where she's standing upfront.

Why did she have to be the TA for this class?

I sit down next to Kingsley and open my laptop. "Is she giving class today?"

"Yep, we're fresh out of luck," Kingsley mumbles, but then a wide smile stretches over her face. "There's a party this Saturday. You're coming, right?"

"A party? I haven't heard anything."

"Just a soiree the Academy hosts, but it will be nice to mingle with everyone."

"Yeah, this place can use a party. It's only been two weeks since classes started, and I'm ready for summer break again."

"You and me both," Kingsley chuckles.

Serena begins the class, and even though I don't like her much, I have to admit she's good at presenting the lecture.

When the lesson comes to an end, Serena says, "Have your assignments in the Friday before Thanksgiving. It will count twenty percent toward your final mark." Her eyes sweep over the hall, then stop on me. "Layla, come see me."

Noise fills the hall as all the students get up. I glance at Kingsley. "Why would she want to see me?"

Kingsley gets up and places the bag strap over her shoulder. "I have no idea. I'll go order food for us, so we can eat outside. Meet me in the park behind the pool house."

"Okay." When she starts to walk toward the aisle, I quickly add, "Get me a chicken sandwich, please."

"Got ya." Kingsley waves then takes the stairs down.

I reluctantly pack my things in my bag before I go down to where Serena's waiting. Stopping in front of her, I wait to hear what this is about.

She crosses her arms over her chest and lets her eyes travel over the length of me before saying, "We haven't had time to talk. I've asked about you in my social circle, but no one knows of you. Who are your parents? How did you get into Trinity? Why do you have a room in The Hope Diamond?"

I blink a couple of times as she fires one question after the other at me.

"This is why you held me back?" I ask. "I'm sorry, but I don't know you well enough to discuss my personal life with you."

Feeling annoyed, I begin to walk toward the exit, when Serena calls out, "I get a feeling you're hiding something, and I will find out what it is."

"Have fun with that," I call back then walk out of the class.

Damn, I wasn't expecting her to be so confrontational. What if she finds out I'm only here because Mr. Reyes gifted me the opportunity?

When I leave the main building, I see Falcon and the guys standing by a sports car. I rush over to them, needing to make sure they'll keep my secret.

"Guys?" The three of them glance at me at the same time, but Lake's the first to smile. I look around to make sure no one else will hear, then ask, "I just wanted to make sure you won't tell anyone who my mother is. You'll keep it a secret, right?"

"What's in it for me?" Mason asks, leaning back against the car. Honestly, I'm starting to think I imagined Mason being nice to me the night of the attack, and that my first impression of him was right. Who is he really? The asshole or a nice guy who's only hiding behind a façade to keep people at a distance?

Falcon shoves Mason against the shoulder, and with a scowl, says, "Go lean against your own car."

My eyes move to Falcon, and I can't help but remember our encounter at the pool. I'll never forget his abs, or his golden skin, or those muscles, or... damn, he was a picture of perfection.

Shaking my head and clearing my throat, I quickly avert my eyes before I'm caught staring at him.

"As long as you're a good assistant, your secret is safe," Falcon says, making me forget about not staring as I frown at him.

"You're bribing me?" Wow, I didn't see that coming. I thought we were past all of that, and we were becoming friends.

"Ignore Mason and Falcon. We're not going to tell anyone," Lake answers me.

"Thanks, Lake," I say, and feeling confused from the hot and cold behavior I'm getting from Falcon and Mason, I walk toward the park where Kingsley is waiting.

That didn't help at all. Now I'm more worried about my secret than before I asked them.

The rest of the week went by without anything out of the ordinary happening, which I'm super grateful for. I'm back into my routine, and I haven't heard any more rumors about Grayson's leaving or about the so-called relationship Falcon and I have.

Yeah, right. If anything, he's only been ordering me around more. Every single day I have to run to the library for him, and at the rate he's ordering coffee, I'm pretty sure he's going to overdose on caffeine soon.

My phone beeps where it's on my dresser, but I first finish pulling on my jeans before checking it.

Come shine my shoes.

I swear I can feel my one eye starting to twitch as my temper sizzles to life.

Shine his damn shoes? What the hell do I look like?

"Yeah, I was wrong. He's still a jerk," I grumble as I shove the phone into my pocket and leave my room so I can go up to his suite.

After getting in the elevator, I scowl at the numbers as they climb higher.

I seriously need to talk to Falcon about this assistant thing. It's starting to interfere with my study time.

Stepping out, the frown on my face grows with every step closer to his door. By the time I reach his suite, I'm so damn annoyed, I bang on the door.

The door's yanked open, and Mason glares at me. "What crawled up your ass?"

I take a deep breath, trying hard to reign in my temper while I match Mason's dark look with one of my own. I don't bother answering him and step inside the suite.

"Just shine them here. I need them in ten minutes," Falcon says while coming out of a room on the left side of the suite.

My lips part and I forget to blink when my gaze lands on him.

It's moments like these I wish I had a photographic memory. *Bare chest. Snap. Suit pants, unbuttoned and hanging loose on his hips. Snap. Snap. Bare Feet. Snap.*

Sigh. He might be a jerk, but he's one hell of a hot jerk.

"Layla?" Falcon slightly tilts his head, and the corner of his mouth begins to lift.

Ugh, then he adds the sexy smirk.

I begin to blink rapidly and glance around the room. "Where are the shoes?"

Falcon gestures in the direction of the lounge, and I notice the brown leather box on the coffee table.

"Don't scratch them." With the warning, Falcon goes back into his room, giving me a quick view of his well-toned back.

Damn, those shoulders.

Mason lets out a chuckle while closing the door. "You have some drool there."

"Huh." I glance up at him with a frown and stupidly wipe over my mouth with the back of my hand before I realize he's pulling my leg.

Well, that wasn't obvious at all. Way to go, Layla.

I sit down on the couch and pull the box closer. When I take the lid off and see the shoes which don't have a speck of dust on them, I grumble to myself, "He's just baiting you, Layla. Don't fall for it."

I glance at Mason, and when I see him smirking at me, I pick up the one shoe and make a show of blowing the invisible dust off it, before doing the same with the other shoe.

I cover the box and get up. "All done." Waving at Mason with a smile on my face, I walk right by him and let myself out.

After having to clean Falcon's already pristine shoes, which must cost more than my entire wardrobe, I'm not really in the mood for a party.

I'll just make an appearance for Kingsley, then go crawl into bed and binge-watch a show.

I take the short route to the main building, past the back of the library. The second I step onto the paved path a couple of meters from the entrance of the hall where the party is being held, I come to an awkward halt.

A girl glides past me, dressed in nothing short of a ballgown. As my eyes flit from one student to the next, I gulp because they're all dressed in formal wear.

Ahh...

Shit.

I hear someone laughing to the right of me, and feel like dying of mortification when I see Lake and Mason walking my way.

"Don't laugh," I scold them. "I'm dying of embarrassment here."

Stopping next to me, Lake places an arm around my shoulder. He presses his lips together, and his eyes begin to water from the effort to not laugh right in my face.

"That's not any better," I complain.

He throws his head back and laughs so damn hard, it draws unwanted stares in our direction.

"Stop, Lake," I hiss under my breath, lightly slapping him on the chest.

He finally contains himself, then pulls me along as he begins to walk back to the dorms. "You're so damn adorable. Come on, I'll be your fairy godmother for tonight."

"While the two of you play dress up, I'm going to find something stronger than the damn coffee Falcon has been shoving at me all week," Mason grumbles.

I don't get to ask Lake what he's planning because he pulls out his phone and begins to make various calls. We reach The Hope Diamond just as Kingsley comes out of her dorm.

"Layla," she calls and waves at me before she crosses the road. "Why aren't you ready? We're going to be late."

"I was ready," I mutter. "You didn't tell me it's a formal event."

"But..." Kingsley frowns, looking baffled, "I said it's a party."

"That back there," I jab a thumb over my shoulder in the direction of the hall, "is a formal event. Where I come from a party is casual with drunk students doing stupid things they regret the next day."

Once the words are out, I realize my mistake.

Kingsley frowns and asks, "Where are you from?"

"Let's get Layla changed first, then you can continue the conversation," Lake tries to save me.

The three of us go up to the suite, and while we wait for whoever Lake called to arrive, I decide to be honest with Kingsley. She's earned my trust over the past couple of weeks, and I'm sure she won't judge me.

"Kingsley," I sit down next to her on the couch, and turn slightly toward her, "I want to tell you something."

"Sure." She smiles brightly as if she's already forgotten our conversation from ten minutes ago.

"My mom is a PA for Mr. Reyes, and my dad is a... ah, let's just say he's a travel blogger. I don't come from a

134

wealthy family. Mr. Reyes gifted me the opportunity to study at Trinity," I blurt the truth out before I lose my nerve.

Kingsley remains quiet for a moment, and it's not helping the anxiety I feel.

"Okay," she finally responds. "I don't care about stuff like that, but I can see how it can be a problem where the other students are concerned."

"Especially Serena," I mention.

"Yeah, especially her. We'll just have to make sure she doesn't find out," Kingsley agrees, then adds, "My family hasn't always been wealthy, so I'm the last person who will judge anyone because of their bank balance."

"Thanks, friend." I reach over and give her hand a squeeze, appreciating her even more than before we had the talk. A knock at the door ends the conversation, but I have to admit, I feel tons better not keeping it a secret from Kingsley anymore.

Lake goes to open the door, and soon the suite looks like it's being converted into a fashion house. Kingsley claps her hands like a little girl, her eyes sparkling with excitement.

She lunges forward and grabbing the dress hanging closest to her, she swings around and shoves it into my arms. "Try this one first."

My eyes bulge as I take in all the dresses. "I'm not going to try them all on. We'll be here all night."

"True," she agrees, and biting her bottom lip, she begins to take a closer look at each dress. Picking another three from the wide selection, she lays them over the back of the couch. "Just try these three. Give that one back."

I do as she says and grab the first one. It's silver, and once I've squeezed into it, my eyes drop to my chest. The material hangs so low and loose if I have to bend forward, it will be a free view for all.

I open the door slightly. "Psst... Kingsley." When I get her attention, I gesture for her to come inside.

Just like Lake did earlier, Kingsley presses her lips together to keep from laughing. "Oooh... with a push-up bra, you'll have some serious cleavage."

I begin to shake my head, giving her a no-way-in-hell-look.

"Fine, no showing off the tatas. Let me grab the next dress." She darts out of the restroom, and a couple of seconds later shoves the next one at me.

It's a blush pink ruffles gown, and once I have it on, a smile forms around my lips because it's really pretty. I turn slightly so I can see it from behind. It's laced up at the back, showing off skin, but it doesn't bother me.

I open the door and walking out, I adjust one of the ruffles.

Lake is the first to notice me. "Yep, that one." Holding up a finger, he walks to where boxes line the dining table. "This pair will complement the dress."

"You look gorgeous," Kingsley gushes then frowns at Lake. "Let me see them first." She peeks into the box before looking at Lake with huge eyes. "Damn, you're good. Valentino is always a winner."

Lake lets out a chuckle and walking over to me, hands me the box. I sit down on the couch and taking a heel from the box, I have to admit they are gorgeous.

Four inches. I'm sure I can manage it without falling flat on my face.

The blush color Nappa leather around the edges of the black heel gives it the perfect finish to match the dress I'm wearing.

I slip them onto my feet and carefully get up. After taking a couple of steps, I smile at Lake.

"Beautiful," he compliments me with a warm smile that reaches all the way to his eyes.

"My hair and other stuff okay?" I ask. I didn't do anything fancy with my makeup, and my hair's just hanging in loose curls down my back.

"You really look stunning," Kingsley gives her opinion. "Let's get going, or we'll be very late. I'll let you all out," she says to the team Lake called on for help.

While Kingsley is busy, I walk closer to Lake and placing a hand on his shoulders, I stretch up on my toes to press a kiss to his cheek. "Thank you, Lake. You're always saving me."

"You're welcome." His eyes focus on someone behind me, and I'm assuming it's Kingsley, but then he says, "You're back. Did you forget something?"

Glancing over my shoulder, I see it's Falcon. I feel something ripple through me because he looks devastatingly handsome in the navy tuxedo he's wearing.

"Am I interrupting something?" he asks, his eyes moving from me to Lake.

"No, Lake was just doing me a huge favor," I answer, not wanting any misunderstandings. Looking back to Lake, I smile, "I'll see you at the hall. Thanks again for everything you do for me."

While I walk to the door where Falcon is still standing, Kingsley's head pops up behind his shoulder. "You coming?"

"Yes." Falcon's eyes glide over me, and when he doesn't move out of the way, I stop in front of him. "Can I squeeze by quickly?"

He nods slightly and turns sideways, which means I literally have to *squeeze* by him. The aftershave he's wearing smells so damn good, and I take a deep breath. The hair on my right arm feels as if they're hypersensitive when I brush past him.

Every time I see Falcon, my attraction toward him grows, and I seriously don't understand it because he infuriates me way more than the scarce moments we manage to get along.

Last week when he held me until I fell asleep feels like a distant dream.

Chapter 10

Falcon

Fuck my life, her dress isn't helping.

I've been fighting this damn attraction between Layla and me all week because let's face it, us dating will create one hell of a shit storm. Mother will have a heart attack and Father... I'm not sure what his reaction will be if I date his PA's daughter.

I stare after Layla as she walks with Kingsley to the elevators, and practically drink in the smooth pale skin of her bare back like a drowning man.

"How long do you intend on fighting your feelings?" Lake asks, and leaning against the wall with his shoulder, he crosses his arms over his chest.

"What feelings?" I mumble, my eyes rushing back to Layla. They're waiting for the doors to open, and she laughs at something Kingsley says.

How can someone get more beautiful every time you see them?

Lake waves his hand in front of my face, yanking my attention to him. "What feelings?" he asks, giving me an incredulous look. "I thought we had this talk. Are you still going to deny it?"

"Nope, I'm just going to ignore it," I say, and walking into the suite, I go to my room to grab my phone where I forgot it on my bed.

"Why?" Lake asks the second I come out of my room.

"Because it won't work."

"Why?"

I give Lake a look as we leave the suit. "Drop it already."

Again he begins to form the word with his mouth.

"You know why," I say, stopping him from asking. "I might be giving my mother shit about her wanting me to marry Serena, but bringing a girl like Layla home would be suicidal."

"So, you're going to marry Serena?" Lake asks, and grabbing hold of my elbow, he forces me to stop walking. "We had a deal. I agreed to the arranged marriage. Mason agreed to joining CRC. We did that for you, Falcon." Lake's eyes lock on mine, and I know now is not the time to brush him off or to fuck around. "All you needed to do was focus on getting the new business off the ground."

"I'm not marrying Serena," I say, so he'll stop worrying. Placing my hand on his shoulder, I give it a squeeze. "But that doesn't mean I can marry just anyone."

"Yes, you can. That was the condition. I'm bringing the business deal in with my marriage to Lee-ann. You and Mason don't have to worry about that," Lake argues his point.

He's right, that was our deal when the three of us sat down to discuss our future.

"My parents will never approve of my dating Layla," I voice my biggest worry.

"Since when do you care about their approval?" Lake challenges me.

He has always been able to see right through Mason and me.

"There are so many reasons why not to date her," I admit. "For one, she's Stephanie's daughter. Stephanie will have my balls on a golden platter if I hurt her daughter. Let's also not forget she knows every single thing about us and CRC. I'd be stupid to screw with that."

"Stephanie is a professional, Falcon."

"Layla will become a target. What happened with Grayson will only be the beginning."

"We'll protect her," Lake replies to my worry.

"Who says she'll want to date me anyway?" I begin to scramble for reasons.

"Yeah, you have a point. You've been a bastard the past week. Please, stop with the coffee orders. Mason and I can't drink much more of it."

A smile begins to form around my mouth, but then Lake says, "Do you like her that much?"

I've asked myself the same question so many times since Layla fell asleep in my arms, and the answer is the same every single time. "Yes."

"Then you should give a relationship with her a chance, Falcon. Don't let her slip through your fingers."

I nod, knowing it will be something I'll regret if I let her go.

"But first you'll have to grovel. Flowers, chocolates, cruises, Tiffany & Co." I nod harder and begin to chuckle when he adds, "She's a good match for you. She won't take your shit."

"Like you?" I ask, pulling him closer for a brotherly hug.

"Yeah, and seeing as I'm already taken, she will have to do," he jokes.

***

Somehow, we get to the hall before Layla and Kingsley, even though they left a good ten minutes before us.

We join Mason at our designated table. I unbutton my jacket before taking my seat, then let my eyes scan over the tables again.

"Who are you looking for?" Mason asks, looking bored out of his mind.

"No one," I answer, and reaching for the tumbler in front of Mason, I bring it to my face and sniff. "Whiskey?" I set it down again and lean back in my chair.

"Yes, or I'll kill someone." His eyes go to where West is sitting.

"If it's that hard for you, I'll ask him to leave," I offer.

Mason shakes his head and takes a sip of his drink before saying, "I just hate seeing him breathe." A coldblooded look hardens his features. "The fucker got away with murder."

Lake and I have tried talking to Mason about the accident his sister died in. Logically, it was an accident. It was snowing heavily the night Jennifer lost control of her car and collided with a tree. West also lost control over his car and crashed into the back of Jennifer's car.

Mason knows this deep down because he was in the car with her when it happened, but the loss was too much and way too sudden. Hating West is Mason's way of coping because he's definitely not dealing with losing Jennifer.

"Excuse me," one of the freshmen says, drawing our attention away from West. "Lake, Mason, I noticed you haven't chosen your assistants yet, and I would like to hand in my application for the position. If that's okay, of course."

Mason stands up and taking the half-empty tumbler, he starts to walk toward the balcony. "There's no way in hell I'm subjecting myself to that level of torture. He's all yours, Lake."

At first, the freshman looks like a regular nerd, but when I take a closer look, I see the intelligence in his eyes.

I'd bet my shares this guy is the genius we accepted.

"What's your name?" I ask, and gesture toward an empty chair for him to sit.

"Really?" He rests a hand on the back of the chair, waiting, and when I nod, he quickly sits down. "Thank you.

145

I'm Preston Culpepper. It's such an honor to study at Trinity. Thank you for accepting me."

"You're studying Economics, right?" I ask, and leaning back in my chair, I smile at Preston.

"You know what I'm studying?" Preston asks, looking shocked.

"Yes, but not the reason why."

Lake leans his elbows on the table. "Guys, not to interrupt your budding romance, but I'm the one who needs an assistant." A mischievous smile forms around his lips. "Then again, I could take Layla, and you can have Preston. I don't mind switching."

"Preston, you're Lake's assistant. Congratulations," I say quickly because there's no way I'm giving up Layla.

"Are you guys joking right now?" Preston asks, an unsure look pinching his eyebrows together.

Lake holds his hand out to Preston, who cautiously takes it. "You start tomorrow."

"I got the position?" Preston's entire face transforms from unsure if we're screwing with him to looking like he's about to cry from total elation. "Thank you so much. I'll do my best."

Lake pulls his hand free. "Dude, relax. I'm the nice one out of the three."

"I know, that's what I'm most thankful for," Preston says, looking over-emotional.

"Yeah, I'd want to cry too if I had to be Mason's assistant," Kingsley suddenly says behind me.

"Is that so?" Mason asks as he walks up behind Kingsley.

I'm usually good at reading Mason, but right now, I can't tell if he's joking or pissed off. I get up and go stand next to him just in case.

Kingsley smiles awkwardly as she turns around to face Mason. A nervous look quickly settles on her face when she meets his eyes.

"In that case," Mason grins, which sets me at ease. He never grins while losing his temper, so Kingsley should survive whatever he has up his sleeve.

Mason walks to her and placing a hand on her back, he nudges her forward, while calling out, "Everyone, I have an announcement to make."

Silence descends around us and Kingsley begins to shake her head, her eyes wide on Mason. "No, Mason. I really don't –"

A huge smile spreads over Mason's face. "Kingsley Hunt is my assistant. Let's give her a round of applause."

Mason's eyes are sharp on hers when he whispers, "She is going to need it."

He walks away and begins to move from table to table, talking with the students and leaving me with a dismayed-looking Kingsley.

<hr />

After Mason's announcement, which got everyone's attention, my eyes land on Layla.

'Do you like her that much?'

'Yes.'

'Then don't let her slip through your fingers.'

Layla pats Kingsley comfortingly on the shoulder, and you'd swear Kingsley received a death sentence by the pained looks on their faces.

Well, we are talking about Mason here.

"You'll be fine," I say to her, trying to offer some sort of encouragement.

She starts to shake her head. "No, I won't because he'll expect it of me to be at his constant beck and call, and let's face it, hell will freeze over before that happens."

"I'm sure Layla has a couple of tips for you on how you can win Mason over. She's been doing a great job with me," I say, knowing full well my words will catch Layla off guard.

"I have?" Layla asks, a stunned expression washing over her face.

"What are you talking about?" Kingsley asks, looking totally lost.

I gesture between Layla and me. "We get along well," I lock eyes with Layla, hoping I'm not wrong, "and like each other." I pause for a moment trying to gauge Layla's reaction to my words. She just stares at me with a slight frown on her forehead. Glancing back to Kingsley, I say, "There's hope for you and Mason."

"I'm not so sure about that," Kingsley comments, her eyes boring holes into the back of Mason.

I take two steps closer to Layla and tilt my head slightly to catch her eyes. "About you and Mason or Layla and me liking each other?" I ask.

"About Mason and I not killing each other," Kingsley snaps, then quickly adds, "Ohh... Ohhhh. Shit, I didn't see that coming. Ahh, I'll leave the two of you to talk."

She scurries away from us, and I know I'm taking one hell of a chance by doing this publicly, but it's for Layla. Everyone will know, and if they try to fuck with her, they'll have to deal with me.

"Let's date, Layla."

You can hear a fucking pin drop on the plush carpet. I'm pretty sure I'm not the only one holding my breath as I wait for her to say something.

Chapter 11

Layla

Let's date?

Did Mason tell him I didn't shine his shoes, and now he's taking revenge on me?

Is he pulling my leg?

Crap, I don't know if he's serious or joking.

Everyone is staring at us, and I have no idea what to do. I let out the breath I've been holding along with a nervous chuckle. Needing to defuse this situation, I decide to play along. If it's a joke, then everyone gets their laugh, if not… Nah, I'm pretty sure Falcon is kidding.

"Why not? I don't have better offers right now." I hear the words leave my mouth, and I promise to all that's holy, that was not what I wanted to say.

Yeah, let's date.

Sure, wanna start now?

Of course, I'd love to.

Any of those would've been better. But... I don't have better offers? What the hell, Layla?

I'm just about to start praying for the ground to swallow me whole when Falcon smiles. Like a full-on – sexy in a way which wakes my hibernating hormones – smile.

"That's a yes, right?" he asks, stepping closer to me. He takes hold of my arm that's been hanging next to my side like a limp noodle. Slowly, his touch moves down until he reaches my hand. When his fingers close around mine, it sends tingles rushing over my body like a monster tsunami.

I nod, not able to utter a single damn word right now.

Falcon looks over my shoulder and nods, and soon piano notes begin to fill the room. Keeping hold of my hand, he pulls me toward an open space where a violinist is standing next to a grand piano.

"I can't dance," I whisper urgently. "Falcon!"

He turns to face me with such an intense look all I can do is swallow. He guides my hand to his shoulder before placing his on my lower back, and then he closes the meager distance between us until our fronts are touching. My breaths begin to speed up when he raises our joined hands, and then he takes a step forward.

Oh. My. God.

Falcon holds me so tight, giving him full control over our movements. By the grace of all that's holy, I manage to not mess things up, and when I get used to the pattern of our steps, I actually have a moment to appreciate the music.

Delicate notes drift around me, and it feels as if everything slows down, everything fades until it's just us and the piano piece.

Slowly my eyes drift up until they find Falcon's, and again I forget to breathe.

He was serious.

Falcon was dead serious, and it's written all over his face as he stares down at me.

We get along well… and like each other.

Falcon likes me.

For a moment, while the notes weave a spell around us, happiness flows through me.

But it's only for a moment.

Because he is Falcon Reyes.

And me? I'm just Layla.

Tongue-tied.

Out of my depth.

And as elegant as a baby moose taking its first steps.

Yeah, that about sums up the past hour of my life. I've been trying my best to be social, but ever since the dance, my whole existence feels wobbly.

There's also Serena who somehow keeps popping up in my line of sight, and the glares coming from her is icy enough to save the world from global warming.

And last, but definitely not least… Slowly, I turn my head to Falcon, who's standing next to me. My eyes glide over his side profile. The self-assured set of his shoulders. The cultured smile as he talks with others.

He's a god, and I a mere mortal.

He's a mountain lion, and I'm… a baby moose.

He's Jupiter, and I am Mercury.

He's the kind of man you only dream about because being with him is the end disguised as the beginning. It's the end of your individuality because there is no way your light can keep burning and not be consumed by his inferno.

I don't think I can give up who I am for anyone. Dad taught me to love myself first. Only then will I be able to love someone else unconditionally. If I have to let go of my dreams, who I am, and who I want to become, I'll only end up resenting him.

Sadness sprouts in my heart because the chance to fall in love with Falcon was only a cruel illusion.

"You ready to go?" Falcon asks.

My eyes come back into focus on his heartbreakingly, beautiful face. I nod, and he takes hold of my hand, linking our fingers together. I follow Falcon out of the hall, my gaze glued to our joined hands.

I try to memorize the feel of his skin against mine. I try to remember what it felt like to rest my head against his chest the night he comforted me.

I try.

In the shadows between two lamp posts, my feet falter to a stop. Falcon turns back to me, and I longingly take one last look at our hands before I pull mine free.

"Did you mean it?" I ask, not wanting to sound like an idiot if Falcon was only joking.

"What?" He asks and shifts to stand in front of me. "About us dating?"

"Yes." I stare at the top button of his dress shirt, not having enough courage to meet his eyes.

"I meant it."

My tongue darts out, wetting my lips, which feel parched. "Falcon, you're an heir to CRC Holdings."

"My family doesn't have a say in who I date," Falcon interrupts me.

He sees right through me with those gorgeous, intelligent eyes.

"We come from two different worlds." I force my eyes up to meet his. "You have a private jet. I like to take road trips. You go to world-class resorts. I like roughing it in a cabin. The suit you wear costs more than all my belongings combined. But I love my belongings. I love my down-to-earth life."

A breeze picks up and blows some of my hair across my neck. Falcon reaches for the strands, and his knuckles graze against my neckline as he brushes it back.

"That's one of the things I like about you, Layla. There's no pretense. You never hesitate to show what you're feeling. You have spirit, and I don't believe you understand the meaning of backing down even when you're outnumbered. The girls I grew up with," he shakes his head, "they'd still be in the hospital after going through the same thing you did. But not you. You defend yourself instead of calling the family lawyer or having your mother deal with the problem."

"I'd probably die kicking and screaming one day instead of just going gracefully," I try to joke.

"Layla," Falcon's voice drops low, and he cups my face as he closes the small distance between us. He tilts my head back, and our eyes lock. The moment is so all-consuming my body matches every breath to his. "My life is black and white, and I didn't know what color looked like until I saw you. I agree we're different, but that doesn't mean I don't want to experience your world."

"I really can't see you going on a road trip and staying in a cabin."

"I'll make you a deal," he says, looking so damn serious you'd swear he was busy with a board meeting. "The ski trip this December. Instead of flying there and staying at the resort, I'll let you plan it. If I like it, you have to agree that we can work. If I hate it, I'll agree that we won't make it as a couple."

"You'll let me plan the entire trip?" I ask to make sure we both understand what the deal entails.

"Yes. The whole thing."

"Okay," I agree. "You have yourself a deal, Mr. Reyes." I pull back and hold my hand out to him. A smile tugs at his lips when we shake on it.

Before he lets go of my hand, he quickly adds, "Until then we date." He grins at me. "We shook on it so you can't go back on the deal."

"But."

Falcon turns around and begins to walk away.

"Falcon, wait. That wasn't part of the deal." I try to rush after him, but the stupid heels are slowing me down. Stopping, I take them off then quickly catch up to him as he walks into our building. "Whoa, hold up," I say as I dart around him and block his way with my arms wide to the sides, a shoe in each hand. "You don't think we need to talk about our dating? This morning I was your assistant." Scrunching my nose, I remember this afternoon. "Why would you ask the girl you like to shine your shoes?" I put my hands on my hips, frowning up at him.

He points at my face. "To get that look."

"What look?" I try to see my reflection in the windows, but I'm too far away.

"The look where I'm not Falcon Reyes. I'm just a guy who annoyed you." He pauses as his words sink in. "I'm just a guy."

Oh, Falcon.

My heart squeezes painfully for him. He's starved by the restrained life he's been living, and I can't blame him. I'd just shrivel up and die if I had to live the way he does.

"I'm going to show you what it's like to live," I whisper.

"Promise?"

"I promise, so you better prepare yourself for one hell of a ride."

I smile up at Falcon, excited that I'll get to show him the beauty of my world. Cupping my chin, his thumb brushes over my bottom lip. When his eyes drop to my mouth, there's a fluttering in my stomach. Falcon begins to lean down, and anticipation builds between us, making me wish the moment could last forever, but at the same time wishing he would kiss me already.

"I'm going to wake her up if she's sleeping," I hear Kingsley's voice.

We pull apart, and in my attempt to look for my keycard, I drop the damn shoes causing them to land with a clatter on the floor.

"You're throwing the shoes? Why?" Kingsley asks.

"Dropped them. By accident." My breaths are coming way too fast, and Kingsley notices because she begins to grin.

"You two need another minute to finish what we interrupted? We can go back out. Right, Lake?"

"We can walk around the building," Lake adds.

"Fuck that, I'm tired," Mason grumbles.

"Mason!" Kingsley complains.

"What? Her room is right there. They can go inside," he argues as he walks to the elevators.

"I left my keycard in your suite," I mention while pointing up. "I'm going up to grab it."

We all join Mason in front of the elevator, and Kingsley mumbles under her breath, "Romance killer."

I feel Falcon's hand brush against mine, and then his fingers link with mine.

When the doors slide open, we all step inside. While we go up, I can almost believe our little group can somehow fit into each other's lives.

Mason with his temper. Kingsley with her humor and sass. Lake with his warmth. Falcon with his bravery to fight for the life he wants. And me? I'll be their rainbow.

Chapter 12

Falcon

We all step into the suite, and reluctantly I let go of Layla's hand so she can go change into her jeans and shirt she left here earlier.

"Is there any food up here?" Kingsley asks.

"Why are you still here?" Mason slumps down on the couch and gives her an annoyed look.

"I'm waiting for Layla," she answers, then looks hopefully at Lake. "Any food?"

Smiling, Lake shakes his head. "I can order something?"

"No, it's okay. I have a stash of candy in my room."

Layla comes out of the restroom with the dress hanging over her arm. "Thank you, Lake. I'll have the dress dry cleaned before returning it."

Lake gives her a puzzled look. "Why? It's yours."

"Mine? You didn't rent it?" Layla's eyes lock on Lake, and I wish I could tell Lake to take cover.

"Why would I rent it?" Lake asks while sitting down on the opposite couch from Mason.

"Laaaaaake," Layla groans. "Why did you buy the dress? It must've cost half an arm and a kidney. Can't I return it?"

Lake's face instantly transforms into a look closely resembling an angel. My eyes dart between the two wondering if Layla is going to be immune to the look. Many have tried and failed. Hell, the look even works on Mason.

"Please keep the dress. It's a gift."

Layla blinks at Lake a couple of times, but then she lifts her chin. "I really can't. It's too much for a gift, and I don't go to many places where I can wear it."

I press my lips together to keep from smiling.

Mason turns slightly and holds up his hand. "Woman, high five. You either have a heart of stone or way more will power than I gave you credit for."

Layla looks baffled as she frowns at Mason and hesitates before she slaps his hand. "Not sure why we're high-fiving, but okay."

"Lake just tried to use his superpower on you, and it didn't work. We all fail. Repeatedly," I explain.

"Are you talking about the adorable innocent look he just had?" Layla asks, then narrows her eyes at Lake. "It's cute, but still, I'm not going to give in."

Lake shrugs then takes out his phone. "It was worth a try. I'm ordering pizza. You girls staying or going?"

"Going," Kingsley answers for them totally oblivious to me wanting to spend more time with Layla.

Before I can say something, Layla walks over to Lake and leaning down, she presses a kiss to his cheek. My eyebrow shoots up, and I tilt my head. When Layla turns to Mason, I take a step forward.

Mason turns his cheek while smirking at me. *The fucker.*

"We're not that close yet," Layla chuckles and instead gives him a wave which has me smirking.

"I'll have the dress dry cleaned, then we can return it," she mentions again, and Lake only nods because he's already on a call for food.

My eyes lock on Layla as she walks toward me. She gives me an awkward glance, not looking too sure about how she should say goodnight.

Our first kiss will definitely not be in front of this bunch. I lift my hand and slide it behind her neck.

"Have a good night. I'll see you tomorrow." Leaning down, I press my mouth to her forehead. I take a deep breath of her soft floral scent before I pull back.

I open the door and have to bite my bottom lip when a blush colors the apples of Layla's cheeks. She grins and with a quick wave, darts past me and out the door.

I lean to my right and watch the girls walk down the hallway. Layla waves again as she steps onto the elevator, and we keep eye contact as the doors close.

"Fuck," Lake snaps as I close the door.

"What?" Mason darts up and around the coffee table to get to Lake. He looks at the phone to see what has Lake cursing. "Shit, that's not good."

Worried, I go to stand behind the couch and placing my hands on the back, I lean down.

Starry, Starry Eyes.
Is Falcon Reyes off the market or still available?
Follow us to find out who the mystery girl is
in our next edition.

The headline accompanies a photo someone took while we were dancing. Luckily it shows Layla from behind.

"It's trending," Lake grumbles.

I was hoping to have more time with Layla before the news got out, and the paparazzi started to close on us like vultures.

"I'll call PR and have them take it down," Mason grumbles, and he begins to pull his phone from his pocket.

"It's okay." They both turn to look at me. "It will get out sooner or later. If we try to hide it, things will get worse. The press can't get onto the campus. I'll send out a warning to the students tomorrow. If any of them take photos of us, they'll be expelled."

"If I don't kill them first," Mason growls.

I'm busy picking a watch from my collection when there's a knock at the door.

"I'll get it," Mason calls out.

After making my selection, I close the drawer, and while strapping the *Vacheron Constantin* onto my left wrist, I walk out of my room.

"Falcon, stop with the coffee already," Mason yells, and turning away from Layla, who's holding the usual three coffees, he sees me and scowls, "You're killing me." He pulls his phone out and then sends a voice note as he walks back to his room, "Kingsley, get your ass up here. I have an assignment for you to type out."

Walking toward Layla, the corner of my mouth lifts. "Morning." I take the coffee holder from her and go to place it on the table. "You don't have to bring us coffee anymore."

"Why? The Barista just managed to get your order right. Do you want something else?"

I shake my head as I walk back to her. When I wrap my arms around her, she lets out a startled, "Oh!" I hug her to my chest and take a deep breath. "Ah… Uhm…" Her hands rest on my sides for a moment before they jump away again.

"Hug me back, Layla."

"Ohh-kay," she whispers, sounding uncomfortable. Her movements are jerky, but she wraps her arms around my waist, then stands dead still.

"Falcon," she whispers as if she's sharing a secret.

"Mmm?"

"This is going to take some getting used to," she admits.

"We can stand like this until you're comfortable with the idea." She stiffens in my arms, which makes me instantly smile.

"I have to go into town." She brings her arms to my sides and tries to pull back. I shake my head, tightening my hold. "I need to take the dress to the dry cleaners." I shake my head again. "This is weird. I really didn't think you were the needy kind," she grumbles.

I let out a burst of silent laughter but pull back.

"Do you want to go to town now?" I ask and check the time.

"Why? Did you need me to do something?" she asks.

"You don't have to run around for me anymore."

She narrows her eyes, looking as intimidating as a kitten. "Are you firing me?" Before I can answer, she lifts her chin, "Good, because I was underpaid and overworked."

"Your boss sounds like an asshole," I state, doing my best to look serious.

She actually thinks about it until I tilt my head, giving her an incredulous look.

"What? You were a jerk most of the time," she defends herself.

"Why do you like me then?" I ask, not feeling too confident any longer.

Again, she takes her time to think before she finally answers, "You and Mason are a lot alike. You both have these walls up wanting people to believe you're jerks, but you're not. You didn't hesitate to help me, and it showed me who you really are."

I haven't spoken to her about the attack since it happened. Lifting a hand, I brush over her jaw, where the bruise is covered up with makeup. "I haven't asked because I wasn't sure if you'd rather not talk about it, but is everything healing? Are you sleeping okay?"

She nods then looks down at her feet and shrugs. "It's in the past. I don't like to dwell on things." Wrapping her arms around her middle, she begins to sway back and forth on the balls of her feet.

I memorize all her nervous actions for future reference before I take hold of her arm and pull her against my chest. With my hand on the back of her head and the other around her shoulders, I press two kisses to her hair.

"Talk to me."

This time she doesn't hesitate when she wraps her arms around me, and her hold is much tighter.

"It just scared me. I haven't gone jogging since, and I'm going to pick up a ton of weight with all the candy Kingsley's feeding me."

"Will it help if I go jogging with you?" I ask, tilting my head to the right so I can see her face.

She peeks up at me, and fuck, I'm in trouble when she gives me an adorable look, making Lake's seem like a damn scowl. She nods, and her lips curve into a cute smile.

"I'm going to kiss you senseless if you keep looking at me like that," I growl.

Her eyes widen, and she quickly pulls back. Clapping her hands together, she turns to the door. "Let's get going. I have a class at eleven."

Chapter 13

Layla

This is weird.

So, so weird.

Standing next to Falcon in the elevator, I'm highly aware of every move he makes, every breath he takes, and especially every time his eyes rest on me.

It feels like we've gone from zero to one hundred in the blink of an eye.

"Now, I understand the meaning of being assertive," I mumble under my breath.

"What do you mean?" Falcon asks.

We step out into the lobby and walk to my room. "You're used to getting what you want." I open the door and walk over to the couch to gather my stuff. "I don't mean it in a bad way." I hang the dress over my left arm and shrug my bag over my right shoulder, then turn to

Falcon. "You've never been rejected, so it's easy for you to go all out into a business deal or … ahh… relationship."

Falcon walks over and takes the dress from me. "You've been rejected? By who?"

I frown slightly and begin to count all the times down on my left hand. "First, there was Stephanie from preschool. She didn't want to play with me. Then… yes, how can I forget Ross? He wouldn't accept my mud cakes. Little shit head."

Falcon tries not to laugh but fails. "You have quite a memory."

"They scarred me for life," I state bluntly, keeping the frown on my face.

Falcon shakes his head and placing an arm around my shoulder, he pushes me toward the door. "I'm not falling for it. You've already shown me you don't scar easily. Let's get going.

"Oh, wait." I duck from under his arm and go grab the keys in my bedroom. Twirling them around a finger, I say, "We can't walk to town."

"We're not taking my car?" Falcon asks as I shut the door behind us, and we walk toward the parking area.

171

"No, we're most definitely not taking your car," I say, then I grin up at him. "Lulubelle is sensitive, so don't insult her."

"You named your car," Falcon murmurs, and then he stops walking. "I'm not going to lie, everyone on campus thought that was the janitor's car."

I slap my hand over my heart. "That hurts." I feign looking hurt.

"Is it roadworthy?" Falcon asks, stepping closer to my blue Volkswagen Beetle.

"Now you're asking for a beating," I threaten as I unlock the driver's side. I get in and unlock the passenger door for his royal highness.

Falcon gets in and bundles the dress on his lap. I hold it in, but when my eyes begin to water, I burst out laughing.

Falcon turns in the seat and placing his right hand on my headrest, he leans over to my side. I try to swallow my laughter, but every couple of seconds, it bubbles over my lips. His eyes capture mine, and he begins to lean in.

My laughter dries up, and my lungs forget what their main function is. My fingers wrap tightly around the set of car keys.

His eyes keep hold of mine, and as he gets closer, I can make out tiny gold flecks scattered in his deep brown irises.

A car near us beeps, and then laughter sounds up from a group of students.

Not thinking twice, I grab hold of Falcon's neck and shove him down, trying my best to hide as well.

When I hear the other car pull out, I peek over the dash to make sure the coast is clear. "That was close," I sigh as I sit up again.

Falcon leans back against his seat and covers his eyes with his left hand. His shoulders shake from the silent laughter.

Putting the key in the ignition, I start the car, which has Falcon staring at Lulubelle as if she's an alien lifeform. "I seriously can't remember when last I saw a car that needed a key."

I pull out of the parking bay and wag my eyebrows at Falcon. "Stick with me, and you'll experience all kinds of things."

"Yeah, just not what it's like kissing you by the looks of it," he mumbles.

───────────────

Falcon checks the time again, and it's only been five minutes since we placed our order. When he looks at me, I point to his watch. "You keep looking at the time. Do you have to be somewhere?"

"No, I'm just not used to waiting."

"Patience is a virtue," I quip.

"Do you really believe that?" he asks, leaning back in the booth we're sitting at. "It's from the bible, right?"

I scoot forward and cross my arms on the table, then smile brightly. "It's from a poem. Piers Plowman, which was written by William Langland."

Thank you, Daddy, for teaching me poetry.

"I didn't know that." Interest flickers over Falcon's face.

"Piers Plowman contains the first known reference of Robin Hood." I try to remember the verse Dad told me. "Something along the lines of Conscience teaching about forgiveness, and Patience teaching to embrace poverty."

"Do you agree with it?" Falcon asks.

The waiter brings our order, and I first take a sip of my juice before I reply, "In a way, I do." Not being a breakfast person, I only ordered toast. I butter the slice before I explain further, "I think it should be the other way around, poverty teaching you to embrace patience. You can't do and have what you want with the snap of your fingers. You have to save up and wait to make some of your dreams

174

come true. If everything in life is ready, just waiting for you to take it, it's too easy. There's no joy of finally achieving your goal or experiencing your dream."

Falcon nods with his gaze on something outside the window. "Everything's black and white then with no color," he murmurs deep in thought. Snapping out of the moment, he looks at me and smiles. "You're very insightful."

I shrug and chew the bite I just took. Swallowing, I reply, "Nah, I just have an amazing dad."

"I've never met him." He picks up the cutlery and begins to eat.

"My parents divorced when I was six. My dad's an old soul, and their lives just weren't following the same paths. He's traveling the world. When I'm done with my degree, I'd like to join him."

"Do you take after your father?"

I nod and smile proudly. "My favorite memories of my childhood were the times he came home, and we'd spend the summer vacation in a cabin. He'd tell me about all the places he had traveled to, and what he saw. He'd show me a photo and weave an entire story around it." I let out a happy sigh. "My dad is magical."

Emotion washes over Falcon's face, something similar to pain. Longing?

I watch as he composes himself. "Your father sounds amazing." I wait, giving Falcon time, so he'll tell me what he's thinking, but instead, he points to my half-eaten toast. "Let's finish so we can get back to campus."

Not wanting to force him into opening up to me, I smile and continue to eat. When we're done, and Falcon reaches for his wallet, I shake my head. "I'm paying."

His eyes snap to mine, and I can see he wants to argue. I can't resist taking advantage of the moment to tease him. I get up and walk around the table, then quickly slide in next to him. Placing a hand on the table, I lean in really close to him. When my lips part, his eyes immediately drop to my mouth, and then I whisper, "Thank you."

He frowns. "Huh?"

Struggling not to laugh, I say, "Would it kill you to just say thank you?"

Falcon lets out a burst of laughter and takes hold of my chin, keeping me close to him. His eyes shine with warmth as he stares deep into mine. "Thank you, Layla."

"You're welcome, Falcon."

Wanting to hear him laugh, I quickly close the distance between us, press a kiss to his mouth, then dart out of the booth. I throw cash on the table and walk as fast as I can away from him, and sure enough, his chuckle follows me all the way to the exit.

When we step outside, I grin at him. "You survived eating at a diner. I'm impressed."

"Let's hold off on celebrating just yet. Food poisoning takes a while to set in," he jokes.

"Mr. Reyes!"

Both our heads snap in the direction of the person calling Falcon, but before I can see who it is, Falcon grabs hold of me and shoves me against his chest.

"Back into the diner," Falcon snaps, and I don't have a choice but to move with him, because he's not letting go of me. "How do I get to the back entrance?"

Only when we're rushing down a narrow hallway does Falcon let go of me, but then he grabs my hand. "We have to run."

"Why? Who was that?" I ask, and the worried look on Falcon's face makes me glance over my shoulder to see if we're being followed.

"It's paparazzi. Just keep your head down, so they can't get a photo of your face."

Wait. What?

Stunned, I follow Falcon out the back, and I automatically just run with him. I don't take in my surroundings or where we're heading. I vaguely hear Falcon make a call.

Falcon doesn't want to be seen with me in public?

But he practically announced it to the whole Academy yesterday?

But the press? That's everyone finding out, including his family.

A Bentley pulls up next to us with screeching tires, and then Lake calls out, "Get in. Quickly." Falcon yanks open the back door and shoves me inside before sliding in next to me. He shrugs off his jacket and wraps it around me, covering my head.

Why are there tears burning my eyes?

Why do I feel like less?

Because Falcon is hiding you. You're a secret, Layla.

I shouldn't be hurt. I knew this would happen. Our lives are light years apart. Who was I kidding to think if we really wanted it, we could make it work.

Falcon will marry a trophy wife who will look good on his arm, not the PA's daughter, who got a free ride because his father felt charitable.

Chapter 14

Falcon

That was close. I keep Layla covered, and when Lake drives through the gates of Trinity, I glance at the press vans parked outside.

I shouldn't have let Layla leave the campus. That was a stupid mistake.

Lake parks right in front of our dorm then glances back to us. "Are you okay?"

"Yes, I should've expected it after the article." I open the door and get out. Turning back, I hold my hand out to Layla, but instead of taking it, she gets out and shoves my jacket against me.

Without a word, she begins to walk back towards the entrance, where the press are all camped out.

"Layla," I call after her, "what are you doing?"

She doesn't stop, and when I take hold of her arm, she yanks it away from me. "I'm going to get my car."

I dart in front of her and grab hold of her shoulders, so she won't just walk around me.

She lowers her eyes to our feet, wraps her arms around her middle, and then begins to slowly rock herself back and forth.

Fuck.

"What is it? What's wrong?"

Slowly Layla shakes her head, and when she looks up, the hurt on her face stabs right through me. I've never felt any kind of failure before, but standing in front of this woman, I feel inadequate for the first time.

"I'm an amazing person, Falcon," she whispers, and as she continues, her voice grows stronger. "My parents are proud of me. I'm proud of myself. Honestly, I didn't see it coming. I should've, though. I won't degrade myself to being some heir's secret or side-piece until he's finished with school."

I'm so stumped by what she's saying that she manages to pull free. I stand like a zombie and stare at the empty spot where Layla stood a second ago.

Secret? Side-piece?

Slowly, anger begins to burn in my chest.

Anger at the press. At this world I live in.

And at Layla, for doubting me.

I look up, and my eyes meet Lake's. He must see my anger because he quickly says, "Falcon, give her time to calm down."

I drop my jacket and spinning around, I begin to run. Layla's halfway to the gate when I catch up to her. I grab her hand and pull her the rest of the way.

"Let go of my hand," she grinds the words out. I hear the sob coming from her but keep my eyes on the press. When they notice us, they scramble to start taking photos.

I stop and pull Layla against me. I bring my hands to her face and force her head back, and then my mouth slams down on hers. She brings her hands to my chest and pushes against me, but as another sob forces her lips to part, I tilt my head to the right and let my tongue slip inside.

Layla freezes for a moment, but then her hands move up to my neck. She pushes herself up on her toes, and her tongue begins to dual with mine.

It's our first fight.

It's the first time we've hurt each other.

It's our first kiss.

It's the first time I'm publicly seen with a woman... and it won't be the last.

Layla

It's not like we were actually a couple, so why does it hurt so much?

A stupid tear rolls down my cheek, and I wipe angrily at it.

Did he really think so low of me?

A sob escapes my lips, and it upsets me even more that I'm crying over something which didn't even last a day.

Suddenly, Falcon grabs hold of my hand and drags me behind him. I scowl at his back and try to pull my hand free.

"Let go of my hand," I say, and I hate that I don't sound angry. I try to suppress a sob, but the stupid thing sounds louder than the one before.

Falcon stops and yanks me to him. He takes hold of my face, and then his mouth crashes against mine.

It takes my mind a moment to catch up to what's happening. I've wanted this kiss for the past twenty-four hours. I wanted to feel his arms around me while his lips were on mine, exploring and claiming.

He's finally kissing me.

Wait, hold up a minute. You're angry, remember?

I bring my hands up between us and try to push him back, but another traitorous sob gives him access to my mouth, and the second his tongue brushes over mine, I lose all my resolve to fight.

Falcon.

My soul sighs his name as I reach up so I can get closer to him. I kiss him back, and my heart begins to weave hopes and dreams of having a chance to fall in love with this man.

He lets go of my face only to wrap his arms around me, caging me to his body, and he deepens the kiss. His tongue makes all my thoughts go up in a puff of smoke as it brushes hard strokes over mine.

Soooo gooood.

I slide my arms around Falcon's neck and hold onto him, not wanting the kiss to end. But instead of things heating up like I want, he slows the kiss down.

He pulls back, and when I open my eyes, it's only to meet his burning gaze.

"Don't ever doubt me," he says, and letting go of me, he takes my hand and turns us to face the flashing cameras, which I totally forgot about.

"What's her name?"

"Are you dating?"

"What affect will this have on CRC Holdings?"

"I'll only answer two questions, and then I hope you'll respect my privacy," Falcon states.

He places an arm around my shoulders and pulls me into his side, looking down at me with affection softening his features.

"Meet my girlfriend, Layla Shepard."

Falcon

After giving the press the show they wanted, I practically drag Layla back to the dorm, and once we're in her room, I go stand in front of her.

For a moment, we just stare at each other.

"I wasn't hiding you from the press. I wanted to protect you from them," I explain my actions of earlier. "Now…" I shove a hand into my hair, regretting that I was so damn impulsive, "Now your face is going to be plastered all over the damn country." I turn away from her, my mind racing as I search for a way to fix the mess I've made. "Fuck."

"I'm sorry. I misunderstood," I hear her say. She places a hand on my shoulder and moves in front of me. She makes the same adorable face from this morning, and it melts my heart.

"That's unfair," I growl. "You don't get to look at me like that right now."

She takes a step closer and somehow manages to look even cuter. "I'm sorry, Falcon."

"I'm never going to win an argument between us," I groan.

"Let me make it up to you. We can do anything you want." She smiles and begins to nod enthusiastically. "Anyyyyything."

"And you can't say no?" I ask, really liking the idea.

"Of course, there are certain things we can't do, like murdering someone, eating strawberries because I'm allergic." She pauses to think.

"There's only one thing I want to do," I say.

"Oh? What?"

I take a step closer and bring my hands to her face, gently framing it. Looking into her eyes, the anticipation we've felt the previous times come rushing back. I was scared it would be gone after the impulsive kiss at the front gate.

Layla takes hold of my forearms, her breaths coming faster.

Slowly, I lean down until our breaths are mingling. I never take my eyes from hers, and the current between us becomes charged, causing goosebumps to spread over my body. My heartbeat speeds up when her pupils dilate, and then I press my mouth to hers.

I keep still as my eyes flutter closed, savoring this moment, which should've been our first. Tilting my head, I breathe in her scent. I feel her skin growing warmer under my palms, and then I can't wait any longer. I press my body close to hers, as close as I can possibly get with the clothes between us. Our mouths begin to move, soft and curious until my teeth scrape over her bottom lip. Soft turns to sucking and biting.

Our tongues explore each other, the heat of her mouth driving me to the edge of losing all control. A soft moan from her is all it takes to push me over the edge.

Using my body, I push her backward until she bumps against the wall. For a moment, our mouths separate, and gasping for air, I stare down at her. Seeing her as breathless and turned on as me, has me reaching down and grabbing her thighs, lifting her up against me. Her legs wrap around me, and when my mouth latches onto hers again, I wish there were no clothes between us so I could bury myself deep inside of her.

I get so lost in Layla I forget to breathe. But damn, if I have to die from lack of air, it would be a perfect way to go.

Her fingers tug my hair, and she sucks at my bottom lip, drawing a groan from me.

This is what I've been searching for. This is the one thing I could never buy.

A moment.

A moment where I am her whole universe. She's as focused on me as I am on her, with nothing else mattering right now.

Just us kissing.

Chapter 15

Layla

My hands rub over his shoulders, needing to feel more of him. The kiss grows urgent, our mouths pressing so hard against each other it's bordering on being painful.

But it's a sweet pain that sparks an ache in my abdomen. Something similar to a million butterflies taking flight.

There's a knock on my door. "Layla, we're going to be late for class."

Falcon frees my mouth but doesn't move back. His eyes burn down on me, and I have to clear my throat before I breathlessly call out, "Give me five minutes."

Falcon's breathing is as ragged as mine, his eyes twin infernos. As the heat of the moment fades, emotions crash over me.

If someone had to ask me when was the moment I fell in love with Falcon Reyes, I'd tell them I fell for him when he kissed me as if he was poisoned, and I was his only cure.

"You have to pull away. I'm not strong enough to let you go," he whispers, and it feels as if the words carry a deeper meaning.

I lower my legs and squeeze myself out from the space between Falcon and the wall. With a trembling hand, I try to straighten my hair before I open the door. Blocking the inside of my suite with my body, I say, "I'm going to have to miss today's class. Can you take notes for me?"

A slow smile spreads over Kingsley's face. "Sure. We can exchange notes later, although I bet yours will be much more interesting than mine."

I stick my tongue out at her, which only makes her laugh as she walks away. "Enjoy it."

I shake my head as I close the door and turning around, I lean back against it.

Falcon is still standing exactly where I left him, bracing himself with hands against the wall. I let my eyes glide over the wide expanse of his back, his trim waist, perfect butt, and strong legs.

There's so much power in this man.

Not only is he physically strong, but he has the kind of influence most people can't even begin to imagine.

And me... I'm an eighteen-year-old girl who managed to make him lose control.

For a moment, a dizzying feeling of power overwhelms me. I cover my mouth with a trembling hand as the realization hits hard.

Falcon turns and rests his back against the wall, and when his eyes find mine, I can see he realized the same thing.

"In my world having a weakness is dangerous," he admits, his voice low and hoarse. There's a vulnerability in his eyes, which makes me want to hold him. "You're my weakness."

I shake my head and dropping my hand from my mouth, I rush over to him. I wrap my arms around him and struggle to keep my emotions from overwhelming me.

When his arms remain hanging at his side instead of hugging me back, I look up at him. There's something in his eyes I never thought I'd see... fear.

"I didn't know it would cost so much."

I pull back and wrap my arms around myself. "What?"

"A moment," he whispers. A slight frown forms on my forehead, but then he explains, "A moment of being

190

someone's next breath. Of meaning something more than just this..." He looks like he's about to cry, and it makes my eyes blur with tears. "Something more than this black and white existence."

"What was the price?" I ask, not sure I want to hear his answer.

His eyes lower to the floor, and minutes pass before he looks at me again. "Giving you the power to crush the one thing no one else has access to."

Knowing exactly what he means, I urgently shake my head. "I won't do that."

"That's a promise you can't make, Layla."

"I can," I argue.

"Nothing lasts forever," he whispers, a heartbreakingly sad look flashing over his face.

"Not in your world, Falcon. In mine, there are things that last."

"How can you say that when your parents are divorced?" he asks.

I smile past the sadness I feel for him. "Because they never ended, Falcon. They just got divorced, but they're still good friends. They still share a glass of wine, and my mom will complain about her work, and my dad will complain about delayed flights." A tear slips over my cheek, but I still keep smiling. "My parents still love each other. They never stopped."

"How do you feel about me, Layla?" Falcon asks a resigned look making him come across distant again.

"I like you, Falcon."

The corner of his mouth lifts, but it's only slightly. "That's the problem. I'm the only one who fell." He pushes away from the wall and walks toward the door.

"No. Wait!" I cry, and I rush past him. Blocking the door with my body, I say, "I've fallen."

Falcon closes his eyes for a moment before he opens them to look at me.

"Falcon, I'm in love with you."

He stares at me a while longer, his eyes searching mine for the truth.

"I'm in love with you," I whisper, my throat closing up with everything I feel.

Every painful heartbeat because I realized Falcon hasn't been loved before. He's been given everything, but love.

Slowly, I push away from the door, and I lift my hands to his face. He clenches his jaw as he struggles with his own emotions.

"I'll never use your feelings for me against you."

I promise you this.

"Instead of me being your weakness, let me be your strength."

Please. Please let me show you I'm a loyal person who will never use you.

Taking hold of my hips, he lowers his head until his forehead rests against mine.

"This got serious really fast," he whispers.

I let out a tired chuckle, drained from the intense feelings. "Yeah." I hunch down a little, so I can catch his eyes. "Want to take a nap with me?"

"Yeah."

"Come on." We walk to my bedroom, and I close the curtains.

Falcon lies down on the same spot he did the night of the attack, then holds his arm open for me. I get on the bed and crawl over to him, and lying on my side, I rest my head on his chest. He places his hand on the side of my head, then turns his body into mine while wrapping his other arm around me.

Pressing a kiss to my hair, he whispers, "Thank you." Even though I'm pressed right against him, I still try to snuggle closer. "Thank you for coming into my life."

I'm not someone who cries easily, but now that I've learned how lonely it must be at the top for Falcon, I can't help but cry for him.

And Mason. I now understand why he lashes out so often.

I press my lips together to keep from making a sound as a tear rolls down the side of my face.

And Lake. Sweet, gentle Lake.

My body begins to tremble from all the effort it's taking to not break down and sob.

Falcon tightens his hold on me and presses another kiss to my hair. "It's okay."

I nod, wiping my tears on his shirt in the process.

"I was just overwhelmed. I'm back to normal now. You have nothing to worry about."

I nod again and quickly turn my face into his chest, muffling the sob.

I never knew my heart could hurt so much.

Falcon pulls back and bringing his hand to my face, he wipes a tear away. "Why are you crying?"

"Because it's so unfair," I whisper.

"What?"

"That money robs you of your humanity." Another sob drifts over my lips. "I'm going to be damn mother hen to the three of you now."

"Don't spoil Lake too much, and be careful, Mason might bite."

I laugh through my tears and rest my chin on his chest as I look up at him. "And you?"

He keeps brushing his hand over the side of my face, and the affectionate look from earlier is back.

"I'm going to be needy and require a lot of hugs and kisses."

A wide smile spreads over my face. "Promise?"

"Oh, I definitely promise," he jokes, and pushing me onto my back, he presses a quick kiss to my mouth. He moves a little down, laying his head on my chest.

"Close your eyes," I whisper and bringing a hand to his hair, I softly pull my fingers through the strands. It doesn't take long until his breaths grow deeper.

"I'm going to save you, Falcon," I whisper. "I'm going to save all three of you."

Chapter 16

Falcon

I've spent most of the day catching up on my work. Closing my laptop, I check my watch to make sure I have enough time.

After showering and putting on a fresh set of clothes, I leave the suite. I take the stairs up to the roof and check that everything is in place for Layla's surprise. Luckily, it's a nice afternoon, and there isn't a breeze even though it's overcast. I light all the candles and make sure the snacks I wanted have been brought up.

I quickly go down and knock on Layla's door.

I'm used to having full control over my life, but with Layla – it's both exciting and scary at the same time. I'm experiencing things and feelings I never knew existed, but knowing I can lose it just as quickly, fuck, it's terrifying.

I need to stop thinking about what can happen and focus on what I have right now, but it's easier said than done.

Layla opens the door, and the instant my eyes land on her face, a wildfire of emotion spreads through me, color explodes behind my eyes, and my heart beats easier. I step right up to her and engulf her in my arms, pressing her hard to my chest.

"Uhhhh," she makes a cute face as she strains in my hold while trying to stand on her toes. "Unfair, you're taller," she pouts, and not being able to deny her anything, I press a kiss to her puckered lips. A wide smile spreads across her face, lighting her up brighter than the sun. "Again." I grin and comply, but keep the kiss short. "Again," she whispers, pushing her body a little higher.

Loosening my hold on her, I lift my hands to her face and tilting my head, I softly lower my mouth to hers, then keep still.

Empty and lonely. That was every day before her.

But yesterday, every hour felt different, bursting with everything I thought I'd never have.

Moving my lips, my heart pushes up to my throat, and I latch onto her with an overwhelmingly, fierce need.

And I gain another moment.

197

A heartbeat filled with seasons of color. An instant filled with eternities of touching and tasting the priceless substance of this woman.

Slowing down with the full intention of continuing this up on the roof, I take Layla's hand and pull her door shut behind us.

"My shoes," Layla laughs as I drag her toward the elevator.

"You're not going to need them." My voice is low and thick, and when the doors slide open, I tug her inside.

I push Layla against the wall and crowd her with my body. As I begin to lower my head and the doors start to close, Serena's high-pitched voice slams into my back.

"Falcon, how could you?" I glance over my shoulder and get a glimpse of her angry face before the doors shut.

"Shouldn't we –" Layla begins, but I stop her with a shake of my head.

"I didn't hear anything," I whisper while I lower my mouth to her neck. I suck on her soft skin, my tongue tracing circles around her racing pulse until we reach the top floor.

Layla lets out a moan when I pull back, and it makes a grin form around my mouth.

"Dear Lord, of course, you have to give me that grin as well," she mutters under her breath.

Holding her hand, I lead her to the stairs, and ask, "What grin?"

She points to my face and narrows her eyes. "That grin. The sexy one which makes me forget all the warnings my dad gave me."

"Warnings?" I step out onto the roof, and as soon as she's next to me, I cover her eyes with my hand. Moving in behind her, I wrap my arm around her waist. Leaning down to her ear, I whisper, "Warnings to be careful of guys like me?"

She nods and brings her hands up, taking hold of my arms.

I blow a breath out over her skin and feel a shiver rush through her body. "Who wants to kiss you?"

She nods again before swallowing hard.

"Who wants to kiss every inch of your body?" I brush my mouth over her thundering pulse.

Her body sinks back into mine, and she tilts her head to the side.

"Who wants to leave his mark on your soft skin?"

Layla's breaths rush over her parted lips as I close my lips over her pulse, and I suck hard. When she moans, pushing herself against me, I suck harder, making sure it will leave a mark.

The attraction between us is overpowering. It paralyzes my worries that we're moving too fast and falling too hard. It heightens my need to conquer and seize her, to bury myself so deep inside of her, there won't be space for anyone else.

Wanting to make this night last longer than five minutes, I remove my hand from her eyes and reluctantly turn my face away from her neck.

She opens her eyes and blinks a couple of times before a slow smile spreads across her mouth.

"Falcon." It's a whisper filled with awe.

I drop my arm from around her as she steps forward and watches while she walks through the aisle of candles.

"I didn't think you were the romantic type," she says, turning in a full circle while she looks at all the flickering flames.

"I didn't think so as well," I admit. I walk to where she's standing nearby the blankets I had the freshmen spread out.

She sits down and smiling up at me, she pats the spot next to her. Her eyes are alive with galaxies of dreams.

"Have you ever been addicted to anything?" I ask as I lower myself to my knees.

"No." Her eyes widen. "Have you?"

"Not until now," I admit. I move forward and taking hold of her face, I crush my mouth to hers. I lose myself while sucking, licking, and biting until our lips are swollen, and we're only focused on one thing – consuming each other.

"I'm addicted to how you taste," I murmur against her mouth. I use my body to push her back until she's lying down.

Layla's eyes are clouded with desire as she looks up at me.

A drop of water splats on my hand that's resting next to her head. Another hits my back. "It's starting to rain," I say, but I don't move, sheltering her against the drops.

Layla lifts her hands to my face, and taking hold, she pulls me down. "I don't want you to stop. I want you to continue until you're addicted to more than just how I taste."

I let out a breath, which becomes another as they speed up along with the rain falling down on us.

"I want you addicted to how my skin feels against yours."

Holy fuck.

Layla's magical. She weaves a spell around me until I'm willing to do anything for her.

I move my one hand down to her waist and taking hold of her shirt, I push it up until she arches her back so I can shove it over her breasts. She quickly takes over and yanks the fabric off. Placing a hand on her ribs, I caress her silky skin and lower my head to her breast. I brush my mouth softly over the lace covering her nipple until it puckers into a hard bud, then draw it into my mouth.

The rain comes down in a light shower, and it helps to cool the blazing heat our bodies are creating as we begin to explore each other.

"I want to be inside of you so badly, Layla," I say the words, thinking she's on the same page as me, but wanting to make sure.

She begins to tug at my wet shirt, and I grab hold of the fabric at my neck, yanking it over my head.

Her hands flatten against my chest, and her fingers fan over my skin. "I definitely want the same thing," she says, nodding as her eyes drink in my chest before sliding down to my abs. "Crap, Falcon. You're seriously hot, and I don't mean in an overheating kind of way," she begins to ramble, making my mouth lift at the corner.

I press a quick kiss to her lips to stop her from continuing with her ramble and to focus on the moment again.

She realizes what she was doing and scrunches her nose, looking adorable. I capture her eyes with mine and move my hand up until I cover her breast. A shiver races through her body, and her lashes lower slightly.

I shift down her body and unbutton her jeans. As I pull the wet fabric down her legs, my eyes glide over her body that's shimmering with raindrops.

It's a beautiful sight that robs me of my breath. I make quick work of getting my pants off so I can get back to her. I place my hands on the sides of her hips and press a kiss to the skin above her knee. My tongue darts out, and I lick my way up to her panties. She moves her legs, opening them wider, and the only thing I hate about the rain is not knowing whether she's wet because of me.

I continue kissing my way over her hip and change direction toward her belly button. Taking hold of her panties, I slowly pull them down, and as light brown curls are exposed to me, my mouth begins to water. Growing impatient, and needing her naked, I yank them down her legs, and our eyes meet for the couple of seconds it takes me to remove my boxers while she takes off her bra as well.

Her eyes are focused on my face with such intensity while she slides a hand up and down the length of my arm. Her other hand glides over my neck, and a look I'll never forget settles on her face. The expression is everything I've been feeling. Need and longing.

"I want you, too," she whispers. "I want you so badly, Falcon."

Closing my mouth over hers, I kiss her until my lips tingle from all the nipping and kneading. Keeping myself braced on my left arm, my right hand slips over her abdomen and down between her legs. When I feel the slickness of her desire for me, blood rushes through my veins, and my body heats to the point where I won't be surprised if it turns the raindrops into steam.

Placing pressure on the sensitive area above her opening, I draw a moan from her. I press my forehead to hers, and when the drops trickle down from my jaw, her tongue darts out, catching them. Her hands move to my back, and they slide down to my flanks, where her nails dig into my skin as I enter a finger into her.

Seeing the pleasure bloom on her face and knowing I'm responsible for it, I seriously can't hold back any longer, and as I position my pelvis against hers, I let out a groan. "I didn't bring a condom." I didn't think we'd be tearing each other's clothes off so soon. "I'm clean though. Mandatory checks every six months."

"When was the last checkup?" she asks, and a slight frown forms on her forehead. "It's really hard to focus on being a responsible adult while you keep…" I curl my finger inside her, loving how she loses all track of thought. "Ahh… uhm… I had mine done last month."

"I haven't been with anyone since the last check," I admit, then ask, "Are you on the pill?"

She can only nod as I press my palm down on her clit.

"You okay with me being bare?" I pull my finger out and taking hold of my cock, I rub it up and down her slickness and fuck it feels so damn good, making pleasure shudder through my body.

She nods faster, her nails digging deeper into my back.

I align the head of my cock with her opening and take hold of her hip.

Another moment.

I let my eyes glide over her flushed face then press a kiss to her forehead.

Thank you for giving me this, Layla.

I press another kiss to the tip of her nose, and a soft smile plays around her lips.

Thank you for barging into my life and forcing me to see you.

I press a quick kiss to her lips, then lock my eyes on hers.

Thank you for seeing me and not everything I have.

Slowly, I push inside of her.

Chapter 17

Layla

The expression on Falcon's face as he enters me will forever be one of my most treasured memories.

My body tenses from the slightly uncomfortable feeling until his pelvis presses against mine, and he's fully inside of me.

I've only had sex once, and we were both fumbling teenagers.

Then again, this can't possibly just be sex.

Falcon pulls back, and when he pushes into me again, his eyes burn on mine, and it feels like the first petals of love blossoming between us.

His fingers on my hip tighten and resting his forehead on mine, his lips part as he begins to move faster. Our bodies rock in perfect sync, our breaths mingling while our eyes silently express everything we feel.

When the overwhelming moment of being with Falcon for the first time fades, it gives me the chance to focus on the physical.

I bring my hands up to his shoulders, and I love the feel of his muscles knotting and loosening under my palms as if their mimicking his heartbeat.

His hard chest and abs glide against my skin, and every time he thrusts inside me, his pelvis rubs against my sensitive nerves, causing pleasure to build in my abdomen until my body quivers like a violin string.

The sound of our skin coming together blends with the rain falling around us, creating a perfect song.

Falcon pushes in harder than before, and it makes me gasp. I shift my left hand to his bicep and bring my right to his neck when he pulls out. I feel his body tensing, and I tilt my hips to meet him as he drives forward.

Our breaths mingle faster, our bodies rushing to connect as deeply as possible. The pleasure starting to course through me is so intense all I can do is dig my nails into Falcon. I squeeze my eyes shut and grind my teeth when there's an intense tightening in my abdomen. The feeling is tormenting and incredible at the same time.

"Layla." My name is a breathless whisper on Falcon's lips. I open my eyes to which he whispers, "Don't close them."

A painful look tightens his features before it changes into the most heartbreaking expression. The drops dripping from his face could be tears for all I know.

Falcon's movements change from fast and powerful to remaining sheathed inside me as he crushes his pelvis against mine. My breaths falter for a moment, then a moan slips over my lips, and my body shudders as an incredible sensation surges through me.

Through my orgasm, I see wonder darkening Falcon's eyes, intensifying the moment. His body jerks against mine, and he begins to thrust into me again. His movements speed up, each time driving him deeper until he tenses. The arm bracing him gives way, and he slumps down on me. Burying his face in my neck, he continues to shudder as he empties himself in me.

His breaths explode over my skin, and turning my head to him, I press a kiss to his hair. I bring my hands to his jaw and lift his face so I can press a kiss to his forehead, then the tip of his nose, and finally to his parted lips.

Finding his strength again, he pushes his chest off mine and loosens his hold on my hip. He trails his fingers up my side and cupping my breast, he lowers his head until he presses a kiss above my nipple.

He drops kisses on my skin, working his way to my neck and over my jaw. His eyes find mine, and he whispers, "I'd give everything I have to be able to stay inside of you."

I smile at him. "I've never thought about taking in a permanent resident." My smile quickly turns to embarrassment, and I begin to ramble, "Crap, I sound like a hoe. I didn't mean it that way." When I see that Falcon is struggling not to laugh, I add, "Trust me to ruin a romantic moment."

He shakes his head and smiles wide. "No, your rambling makes it perfect."

After the rain stopped, I scattered our soaked clothes over the roof. While I was hiding under a wet blanket, Falcon snuck down to his suite to get us dry clothes. His sweat pants are way too big, and I'm drowning in his shirt, but it works for now.

Sitting between Falcon's legs, I lean back against his chest. His chin is resting on my shoulder, and his arms are wrapped around me as we look at the distant hills and valleys.

This is perfect.

I look up at the parting clouds, and when the sun breaks through, I point a finger at the sky where a faint rainbow just formed. "Look."

We stare at it, and then Falcon whispers, "That's exactly how I would explain the past couple of weeks of my life."

"A rainbow?"

He shakes his head. "First, the clouds and then the rainbow."

Turning my head, I grin at him. Wrapping my arms over his, I link our fingers.

"Are you a night or morning person?" I ask.

He thinks before he answers, "I'd say a mixture of both. And you?"

"Both, but God helps the person who wakes me up while I'm sleeping." After a couple of minutes passes, I ask, "Are Mason and Lake your only friends?"

Nodding, he says, "They're my family."

"Don't you get along with your parents?"

"No."

I can't imagine something like that. I've never even had a fight with my parents.

"My father spends all his time at work. He's actually just a stranger." I keep quiet, hoping he will tell me more, and eventually he does. "Clare Reyes only cares about one thing, her status. I used to get along with Julian, my older brother, but things have become so competitive between us. I sometimes wonder whether the memories I have of us aren't all just wishful thinking."

"And Lake's parents? Do you get along with them?"

Falcon nods. "Lake has the best parents out of the three of us."

It makes me happy to hear that.

"And Mason? Is he in a similar situation as you?"

Falcon shakes his head, and minutes pass before he says, "They were like Lake's family, but after Jennifer, Mason's older sister, died in a car accident, the Chargills fell apart. Mr. Chargill works until he falls asleep at the desk. He seldom goes home."

"And Mason's mom?"

"She's in and out of rehab."

I close my eyes as empathy for Mason fills my heart.

"How old was he when the accident happened?"

"Seventeen. Jennifer collided with a tree. She died when West's car crashed into her from behind. Mason blames West."

"Is that why they fight a lot?"

Falcon nods again, and I wonder if there isn't a way to help Mason. All that anger and hurt is destructive, and he might end up doing something bad.

"Tell me about you," he murmurs.

"What do you want to know?"

"Who are your friends? Are any of them guys?"

I let out a chuckle. "Kingsley is my first real friend."

Falcon shifts me to the right so he can look at me. "Why?"

"I had a lot of acquaintances, but I don't think any of us kept in contact after school ended. We only spent our breaks together."

For a couple of minutes, we watch the sun setting, then I ask, "Are you joining CRC when you're done with your studies?"

"No."

I'm getting used to Falcon pausing before he answers.

"The three of us made a deal with our parents. Mason will join CRC, and I will start a new company. My father is still trying to get me to join CRC, but that won't happen."

"Because of your brother?"

"Yeah, besides, Julian has the majority shares for our family."

"Does that bother you?"

He shakes his head. "I have Mason and Lake. Our shares combined out votes everyone else."

"So Lake will join CRC as well?"

Falcon doesn't answer the question and instead says, "Lake deserves someone like you more than I do."

I glance back at Falcon.

"Lake's already engaged. The wedding is set for next summer."

"Don't you like his fiancé?" I try to remember if any of them have ever mentioned her, but there's nothing.

"I've never met her," Falcon admits. "It's an arranged marriage."

"What?" I sit forward and turn so I can face Falcon. "Why?"

"One of us has to marry her." Falcon's words send shock rippling through me. "We talked about it a lot before we made our decision. Mason would be the best person to work alongside Julian. I made my first million when I was nineteen, and because of it, it's my job to get our company off the ground."

"And that left Lake," I whisper.

Falcon nods and tries to smile. "He seems okay with it. I've overheard them talking on the phone, and it didn't sound awkward. I'll only know for sure when I see them together."

"You and Mason are both very protective of Lake," I mention. "I understand why, though. I want to protect him, and I've only known him a couple of weeks."

"I'd kill for Lake and Mason."

The statement sounds harsh, but I hear the loyalty behind it. They have an unbreakable bond, and it makes me feel better that they have each other.

Chapter 18

Falcon

"It just took on a life of its own." Mason, Lake, and I are sitting in our lounge, catching up before we head to bed. "The one second I was still realizing I like Layla and the next…"

"She became important to you," Lake completes my sentence.

I nod while staring at all our feet, resting on the coffee table. "This isn't very comfortable, yet we do it every time we sit here."

Mason frowns and glances up from his phone. "What?"

"Our feet on the coffee table. The damn thing is hard," I explain.

"We should get something softer," Lake agrees.

"Kingsley will be lying there if I have my way," Mason growls before he tosses his phone to the side.

Lake coughs to cover up a laugh, and I chuckle and ask, "Is she ignoring your texts?"

Mason shakes his head, a dark frown on his face. "It's only a matter of time before I kill her."

Silent laughter escapes me. "I remember thinking the exact same thing about Layla."

"Now you're killing her with –" I throw my phone at Mason because it's the only thing I had nearby.

"Shut up," I growl.

Picking up my phone, Mason unlocks it.

"There's nothing in there," I warn him.

"I'm texting Kingsley, and God help that woman if she reads your message."

Lake starts to laugh, giving up on trying to hide it.

"She fucking read it," Mason exclaims. He dials her number and puts the phone on speaker.

"Hey, Falcon," Kingsley answers. "Layla's in the shower. Are you looking for her?"

Taking my feet off the table, I sit forward. "She's in the shower?"

Lake begins to laugh again.

"Getting Layla's shower schedule can wait," Mason snaps. "Hunt! What the fuck? How dare you ignore my messages?"

A loud sigh comes over the phone. "Mason, we aren't sleeping together, and you sure as hell aren't paying me, so seeing as you're not my sugar-daddy, I'll read your messages when I have some spare time."

I cover my face and fall back against the couch as I crack up because that's the best comeback I've ever heard. When Lake grabs his stomach and falls off the couch, I practically start crying.

Even Mason has a smile on his face. "You want me to be your sugar-daddy, Kingsley?"

"Oh, God," Lake wheezes. "Can't... breathe."

"Layla, heeelllppp," Kingsley yells.

"What's going on? If it's another spider, I'm burning this place down," Layla's voice comes over the line.

She must hear us laughing because soon her soft chuckle drifts over the phone, then she asks, "Are y'all picking on Kingsley?"

"No, just Mason," I quickly answer.

"Hold up," Mason says. "Kingsley still needs to answer me."

"What did he want?" Layla asks.

"Whether I want him to be my sugar-daddy," Kingsley grumbles.

Layla sounds stunned when she says, "Oh... wow... I so did not see that coming."

"I'd rather drown myself in the bathtub," Kingsley mutters.

"I left clean towels in the bathroom for you."

"Kingsley is going to bathe now?" Mason asks as he gets up, which has Lake scrambling up from the floor and me darting up.

"Yes, so you guys –" Mason cuts the call, and when he runs to the door, we set after him.

He ignores the elevator and takes the stairs, and it has Lake groaning, "Why am I even running after him?"

"To see what he does next," I answer.

Mason gets to Layla's door first and bangs on it. Lake tries to stop but begins to slide because the idiot's wearing socks.

He slams into Mason as Layla opens the door, and they both go tumbling into her room, and it has me sinking to my knees with laughter.

"Did you hang-up on me?" Layla tries to scowl, but when she looks at me, she covers her mouth and turns away, laughter bursting from her.

Mason climbs to his feet and walks into Layla's room.

A moment later, Kingsley yells, "What the hell, Mason!" Followed by a shriek echoing through the suite.

When Mason comes stalking out of the room with Kingsley tossed over his shoulder, I claw at the wall to get to my feet.

"What if I was undressing?" she shrieks at him.

"Then I'd be carrying your naked ass out of this suite," Mason growls.

"Layla, help!"

Mason stalks out, and when Kingsley sees us all laughing, she scowls. "Some friends you all are!"

Lake, Layla, and I have to jog to catch up to Mason as he heads in the direction of the pool house.

When Kingsley realizes where they're headed, she begins to slap his back. "Put me down! Mason, don't you dare throw me in."

Nearing the pool, Mason starts to run, and then he jumps, taking Kingsley with him.

The second their heads break through the water, Mason growls, "You'd rather drown, right?"

Kingsley sputters and tries to doggy paddle away from him, which has Mason tilting his head and asking, "Can't you swim?"

"Fuck off," Kingsley snaps before she goes under which has Lake diving in before I can even react.

"Why the fuck are you all panicking? She's in the shallow end," Mason exclaims.

Lake gets to Kingsley and helps her to stand, then he scowls at Mason, "Not cool."

Placing an arm around Kingsley, he checks if she's okay.

"Get Mason out of the pool so I can kill him," Kingsley growls. She sounds fine, which has me relaxing.

"My heart almost stopped," Layla whispers next to me.

Glancing down at her, I see she's still staring at the three in the pool with wide eyes. I place an arm around her and draw her into my side. "Cute PJ's."

"Right? I got them on sale." She looks down at the yellow outfit that's covered with green UFOs.

"What are you all doing?" Serena's voice echoes through the pool house.

"Fuck," I mutter.

Layla sighs while Lake and Kingsley freeze.

Mason, on the other hand, throws his arms in the air. "There goes the fucking night."

Layla snorts and quickly tries to hide it by burying her face against my chest. I press my lips together, and my eyes begin to tear up.

Mason's laughter explodes through the room. "Falcon's crying."

"Seriously, you all need to grow up," Serena sneers.

"It looks like they're having fun," someone else says, and glancing over my shoulder, I see Serena standing amongst a group of girls.

"No, it doesn't," Serena snaps.

"Right," the girl quickly agrees, looking chagrined.

Serena focuses her glare on me. "Falcon, we need to talk."

Will this woman ever give up? "Make an appointment with my assistant."

"Seriously?" she snaps. Walking toward us, she crosses her arms. With a look of disdain on her face, she glares at Layla. "I actually have something to say to your assistant."

Layla turns around to face Serena, and it has me clenching my teeth.

"Do you really think sleeping your way to the top will work?" Serena's eyes turn icy. "Once a whore, always a whore."

"One... two... three... four..." Layla whispers, then nods and says, "I tried counting to ten. It didn't work."

When she slaps Serena, my mouth drops open. Gasps sound up like a damn chorus to the right of me where Serena's group is.

Layla takes a step closer to one hell of stunned Serena, who brings a trembling hand to her cheek. "I'm not the violent type, but don't you dare talk to me like that."

"You slapped me?" Serena asks, then her face transforms from looking incredulous to murderous. "You made a big mistake tonight."

"That's enough," I growl, stepping between them.

Serena's eyes flick up to mine, and the hatred in them actually worries me. Her breathing speeds up as she whines, "You degraded me and offended my parents in front of the entire nation."

Shaking my head, I ask, "How did I do that?"

"Our families were in the middle of talks about a marriage, and we had to learn from the press you're dating that..." Serena points a finger at Layla, "that woman."

Bringing a hand to my face, I pinch the bridge of my nose. "For the last time, I never made any promise of commitment to you."

"Our families were discussing the terms!" she shouts at me, her cheeks flushing red.

"I. Never. Made. Any. Promise. Of. Commitment. To. You," I enunciate each fucking word.

Clenching her jaw, she glares at me until I feel a shiver crawl down my spine.

This woman is unstable.

I don't break eye contact with her, not willing to be the first to back down.

'I'm going to ruin you,' her eyes spit at me.

'Give me your best shot, but be prepared for the consequences,' I silently warn her.

After Serena crashed our party, we all decided to call it a night. When I get back to the suite, and I pick up my phone, it starts to ring.

Mother.

I've been avoiding her calls the past couple of days, and I know she'll just keep phoning until I answer.

I take a deep breath and accept the call. "Mother."

"Come home right this instant!"

"Why?"

"Why?" she gasps and lets out a burst of disbelieving laughter. "Why?" she yells. "How could you do that to us? The photos are everywhere. PR can't take them all down."

I remain quiet and wave at Lake and Mason before walking to my room.

"You have disgraced us all!"

I shut the door behind me.

"And... and.." she sputters through her anger, "With the PA's daughter? Honestly, Falcon. Is this your way of rebelling?"

I sit down on the bed and lie back.

"You will put an end to that ridiculous affair and make a public announcement that Stephanie will have ready tomorrow."

I dart back up. "You had Stephanie write an apology?"

"It's her job, and she knows her place, unlike that daughter of hers."

I hang up on my mother and search for Stephanie's number. When I dial it, I get an engaged tone. I yank my bedroom door open, which has Lake lifting his head from where he's lying on the couch.

"What's wrong?"

"My fucking mother," I growl. Leaving the suite, I take the stairs down again. When I get to Layla's room, I bang on the door.

She opens it and puts her finger in front of her mouth then points at her ear.

"I know, Mom."

Fuck.

I hold my hand out to her, so she'll give me the phone, but instead, she shakes her head.

"Let me deal with this," I snap and grab the phone from her. I press it to my ear and begin to apologize, "Stephanie, I'm so sorry. Please don't write the apology. I won't be making any announcements. And again, I apologize for my mother's behavior."

"Falcon," her voice is calm and smooth as always, "As I was telling Layla, you're both adults. If you want to date my daughter, all I ask is that you treat her well. I have already communicated to Mr. Reyes that I won't be writing an apology on your behalf."

I let out a breath of relief and walking to the couch, I sit down. "Thank you."

"Can I ask one question?"

"Please," I reply quickly.

"Are you serious about Layla?" Stephanie has always been calm and collected, and hearing the tone of worry in her voice, tells me just how concerned she is.

"I am." Glancing up, I lock eyes with Layla, "I'm very much in love with your daughter. I have no intention of ending things between us."

"Your father will not remain silent. You know this, right?"

"I do. I'm prepared to accept all the consequences, whatever they may be."

"I have to warn you. I will not hesitate to remove Layla from the Academy if I feel her life is being upset in any way."

"I'll protect her. I promise."

"I'm going to hold you to that, Falcon. I love Layla more than anything and anyone. Please keep her safe."

"I will, Stephanie."

We end the call, and I suck in a deep breath of air. Looking at my watch, I see it's already past midnight. I stand up and reaching for Layla's hand, I pull her to the bedroom. I pull my shirt off and lay down, holding my arm open for her. She gets on the bed, crawls over and snuggles against me.

Wrapping my arms around her, I press a kiss to her hair. "I'm sorry this happened."

"It's not your fault," she whispers. "Your parents seem really upset from what my mom told me."

"It doesn't matter," I reassure her.

She lifts her head and looks up at me. "It does, Falcon."

I bring a hand to her face and brush my thumb over the swell of her cheek. "Don't worry about any of it. I'll handle my parents."

She stares at me for a little while, then says, "Thank you for apologizing to my mom. You didn't have to, but it means a lot to me."

A smile tugs at my mouth. "Sleep my rainbow."

A huge smile splits across her face. "I like that."

I press another kiss to her forehead then guide her back to my chest.

Long after Layla has fallen asleep, I'm still staring at her.

I'm going to fight to keep you.

I'm going to fight for us.

Even if it means I have to give up everything.

Chapter 19

Layla

Sitting in class, I keep my face as expressionless as possible while Serena presents the lecture. Every couple of seconds, her eyes snap to me, and a chill goes down my spine.

As soon as the class finishes, I grab my bag and rush to the door.

"Layla!" I hear her snap behind me, but I pretend not to hear and dart out into the hallway.

"Wait up," Kingsley calls. I slow my pace, and when she catches up, she grumbles, "That wasn't uncomfortable at all."

"You're telling me," I mutter.

"Anyway, the class is over," Kingsley looks at the positive side. "Are we going to the library? I want to get this project done and over with."

"Yes, let's make a huge dent in it today. I've fallen behind with it the past couple of days," I admit.

Kingsley hooks her arm through mine. "Mmm... I wonder why?"

Letting out a chuckle, I nudge her shoulder with mine. "It was worth it, though."

"Who would've thought you and Falcon would date?"

"If you told me that last week, I would've asked you what drugs you were on," I joke.

"Just goes to show, anything can happen," she muses.

"Yeah? Like you and Mason? Is he going to be your sugar-daddy?" I tease her, which earns me a scowl and a jab at my shoulder.

"Stop, that shit is scary," she grumbles.

As we walk across the lawn which stretches behind the back of the dorms toward the library, I ask, "Why is it scary?"

Kingsley pulls me to a stop and gives me a confused look. "Aren't you scared of Mason?"

I shake my head, "Why would I be?"

She throws her arms in the air. "Oh, I don't know. Only a ka-zillion reasons." She holds out her left hand and begins to tick them off. "His temper for one. He's aggressive. I've seen him punch West into a bloody mess."

"I really think that's all just a smokescreen," I offer my opinion.

Kingsley shakes her head, not agreeing, "If you ever leave me alone with Mason, I'll never speak to you again. He really terrifies the shit out of me. I wish there was a way I could get out of this being his assistant crap."

"Do you want me to ask Falcon?" I offer, hating that Kingsley feels so uncomfortable.

She shakes her head, "They're best friends. I don't want to cause trouble between Falcon and you."

We begin to walk again and wanting Kingsley to feel better, I place my arm around her shoulders. "Don't worry. I've got your back. I won't leave you alone with him."

She gives me a thankful smile. "Thanks, friend."

My phone vibrates on the table next to my laptop. Checking it, I see a text from Falcon.

Want to meet me on the roof?

A smile forms on my face, which has Kingsley whispering, "Falcon?"

I nod, "Do you mind if I go?"

She shakes her head. "I'm going to finish this page then go catch a nap."

"I'll text you later." I pack up my things and hitching my bag strap over my shoulder, I quickly leave the library.

As I go down the stairs, two girls come up, and when they pass me, the one bumps hard into me. I manage to catch myself by grabbing hold of the railing.

Glancing back at the girls, they both give me looks of contempt. "Excuse you," the girl who bumped into me sneers.

Giving them a cold look, I brush them off and walk away.

You're better than them. You're not going to take the bait. No reaction is the best reaction.

"Aaaannnd there goes all my good intentions," I mutter under my breath when I see Serena standing up ahead. She's talking to an older woman, whom I guess is her mother.

I move off the path and onto the grass, fully intended on giving them a wide berth.

"Oh, Layla," Serena says, her voice so damn sweet it's giving me a stomach ache. "Let me introduce you."

I suppress the urge to roll my eyes, and remembering my manners, I plaster a smile to my face and turn to face them.

The older woman's eyes make a sweeping motion over me, and then her mouth sets in a hard line.

Yep, definitely mother and daughter.

With an angelic smile, Serena says, "This is Clare Reyes, Falcon's mother."

Shhhiiiiitttttt.

My heart starts to beat faster while my mind tries to play catch up.

I take a step forward and hold my hand out to Mrs. Reyes. "It's a pleasure meeting you."

Serena leans into Mrs. Reyes, and says, "This is the girl I told you about, Layla Shepard."

Mrs. Reyes glances down at my hand with disdain before bringing her eyes to mine.

Feeling extremely uncomfortable, I pull my hand back.

This is so bad. So very, very bad.

"Serena-dear," Mrs. Reyes practically coos, "let me have a moment alone with Miss Shepard. When I'm done, we can go for lunch."

"I'll go to the restaurant and have them chill your favorite wine," Serena offers.

"That would be marvelous."

Be strong, Layla.

You're Stephanie and John's daughter.

You have nothing to be ashamed of.

Mrs. Reyes begins to walk past me. "Let's sit under the tree. I have no intention of having this talk out in the sun."

I follow her to the wrought iron bench and wait for her to sit down. I lower my bag to the grass but remain standing.

With an uninterested expression, she gestures to the seat next to her. "Sit down. I have no intention of looking up at you."

"I'll stand."

She glances at the library, then her gaze sweeps over the campus, purposely avoiding me.

Don't be intimidated, Layla.

Exasperatingly, she bites, "I'm waiting."

"For what, Mrs. Reyes?" I ask, keeping my tone respectful.

"For what?" she scoffs. "You owe my family and I an apology."

"I'm sorry," I say, and when her eyes snap up to mine, I continue, "but I have no idea what you're referring to."

Her face turns to stone. Taking a good look at her, I try to see a resemblance between her and Falcon. Her hair has been colored auburn, which makes her light grey eyes seem like frozen ice.

They don't look anything alike.

"You will put an end to this ridiculous façade," she demands.

"I still don't know what you're referring to."

With practiced elegance, she rises to her feet.

"Being inane isn't becoming of you," she snaps. "I'm not sure what your intentions are with my son, but I will not idly standby and watch you latch onto him."

I take a deep breath, trying to not let her words get to me.

"I've seen plenty of girls like you. You're young and moderately pretty, and you think capturing a wealthy man will bring you status and fortune. Not my son." She takes a step closer to me and lifts her chin high, haughtily glaring down at me. "You –"

"I care for Falcon." The words leave me in a rush.

"You think you do," she scoffs. "You're eighteen. My son is the prince of your dreams. I can understand how that can make you think you have something special with him."

235

"We do have something special," I state, not willing to stand by while she reduces our feelings to nothing more than whims.

"If you do not distance yourself from Falcon, I will take it as an act of war," she warns.

"I don't want to fight you," I admit. "But I'm not willing to give up on Falcon. I promised him I'll stay by his side."

She glares at me for a long moment, then coldly states, "Then, so be it." She begins to walk by me, but stops and slightly turns her head. "I'll never welcome you into our family. Falcon will marry Serena."

When she walks away, I wait a couple of seconds before I glance over my shoulder. I watch her make her way down the path, toward the restaurant. Poised and elegant.

Bending down to pick up my bag, I notice how my hand is trembling. I hold both in front of me, willing the shaking to stop.

Sitting down on the grass, I close my eyes.

I want to remain strong, even after she's gone, but emotions begin to flood into me.

What am I going to do?

I'm no match for Falcon's parents.

Needing to hear a supportive voice, I pull my phone from the bag and call my dad.

"Hey, kiddo," Dad's lively voice comes over the line. "How's school?"

"Hi, Daddy." I take a breath and force a smile to my face. "School's good. Where are you now?"

"Nam..." The wind blows on Dad's end, making it hard to hear him.

"Where, Daddy?"

"Le... in-ide." I wait a couple of seconds and begin to pick at the blades of grass. "Can you hear me now?"

"Yes, much better. You were saying?"

"I'm in Namibia."

"Where's that?"

"South-West Africa. Kiddo, I wish you were here. I'm camping at the Skeleton Coast. It's... it's awe-inspiring."

"What do you see?" I ask, needing to escape to where Dad is.

"It's brutally beautiful. Vast bone-dry plains for as far as the eye can see. Wreckages scattered like carcasses. The Bushmen called it the land God made in anger."

Tears well in my eyes, and one slips over my cheek. I close my eyes, soaking in Dad's excited voice, which is filled with reverence.

"I wish I was there right now," I whisper. "I miss you, Daddy."

"Layla?" He seldom calls me by my name. "Do you need me to come home?"

I begin to nod, desperately wanting to say yes. "No, Daddy. I'm busy with school. I just wanted to hear your voice. Send me a photo?"

"I'll snap one for you right now. I'll see you for Christmas. I've gathered many trinkets for you."

"I can't wait to see them."

"Look up, Kiddo."

My breath hitches and I struggle not to sob as I tip my head back and look at the blue sky.

"We're under the same sky," Dad says.

"We're under the same sky, Daddy."

When the call ends, I get up and run, leaving my bag behind. I run as fast as I can by the restaurant, up the trail, and only when I reach the lookout point do I stop.

My breath explodes over my dry lips as I desperately stare at the Topatopa mountain range in the distance.

The instant I've caught my breath, I scream. The sound echoes and I imagine it carrying all my uncertainties and despair away from me.

Chapter 20

Falcon

I wait thirty minutes, and when Layla's a no-show, I try to call her again.

The call goes directly to voicemail, and feeling worried, I dial Kingsley's number.

"This better be you, Falcon," she warns as she answers.

"It's me. Is Layla with you?" I take the stairs down to the lobby.

"I thought she was with you," Kingsley says. "I've just left the library, let me try to call –" Kingsley pauses, and a couple of seconds later says, "Her bag is at a bench next to the library." There's another pause. "I don't see her. Maybe she went to the restroom?"

A bad feeling settles hard in my stomach as I walk out of the building. This is not like Layla.

Knowing Kingsley is to my left, I turn right. "I'll check the restaurant. Let me know if you run into her."

"Will do. Don't worry too much. I'm sure she's somewhere around here."

Cutting the call, I shove my phone into my pocket and walk faster. Students scatter from the path when they see me coming, and when I open the door, stepping into the restaurant, my worry turns to fear. Seeing my mother dining with Serena, anger begins to simmer in my chest. I stalk over to them and coming to a stop next to the table, my mother looks up, then a fake smile pulls at her mouth.

"Falcon, what a surprise."

"It can't be much of a surprise seeing as I go to school here," I reply cynically.

"Nevertheless," she points to the empty chair in front of me. "Why don't you join us?"

Ignoring the invitation, I ask, "What are you doing here?"

Mother picks up her wine glass and takes a sip before answering, "I think it's self-explanatory. I'm having lunch with Serena."

Fuck this. We can go in circles all day long, but it won't help me find Layla.

Without another word, I stalk away from their table. Once I'm outside, I feel the cold grip of fear squeeze at my heart.

Did my mother confront Layla?

Did she manage to drive a wedge between us?

My phone rings and I hurry to pull it from my pocket. When it shows Stephanie's office number, my heart begins to pound in my chest.

"Stephanie," I answer, praying to the gods she's not going to tell me to leave Layla alone.

"Afternoon, Falcon," her professional voice comes over the line, making my heart squeeze painfully with fear, "Please hold for Mr. Reyes."

Fuck. Fuck. Fuck.

This is bad.

She transfers the call, and then my father's voice comes over the line, "I have ten minutes. Explain yourself."

"There is nothing to explain, Sir." I move to the side of the restaurant for some privacy.

"What is this I hear about you and Layla Shepard?"

"We're dating," I answer honestly.

I hear him let out a heavy sigh. "You're young, and the urge to spread your seed can be overwhelming. I understand that, but we do this discreetly."

Closing my eyes, I clench my teeth, so I don't end up cussing at him.

"Your mother is very upset," he lets out another sigh, "and I don't have time to listen to her nagging. Cut ties with the girl."

"With all due respect, Sir, I can't comply with your request."

"Falcon, I will not hesitate to cut you off," he threatens.

"If you feel that's what you have to do." I bring a hand to my face and pinch the bridge of my nose. "I'm capable of providing for myself."

"Unfortunately, that's true," he acknowledges much to my surprise. "You leave me no choice. The Academy will be instructed to remove Miss Shepard from the premises."

Anger detonates behind my eyes, blinding me momentarily. "Do so, and I leave with her. I will marry her and gift her my shares as a wedding present. Don't threaten me, Father," I grind the words out. "You forget, I'm your son, which means I've learned every possible way of warding off a threat." I take a breath, and finish by saying, "Unless you want to see Layla in every board meeting, by all means, carry through with your threats."

I cut the call and feeling like a caged animal, I stalk back to the dorm. I bang on Layla's door, but she doesn't open. Rushing back outside, I try to think where she could've gone.

Deciding to check if her car is still here, I jog to the parking area, and when I see the blue beetle, I let out a breath of relief.

"She has to be on the campus," I mutter as I head back in the direction of the dorms. As I pass them, and I'm just about to walk toward the academic buildings, I see her as she walks by the restaurant.

I begin to run toward her, so fucking relieved to finally see her. Her eyes land on me, and she stops. I slow down and slamming into her body, I wrap my arms around her.

"Fuck, I was so worried."

Her arms move around my waist, and her hands grab hold of my shirt. "I'm sorry for worrying you," she whispers.

Pulling a little back, I bring my hands to her face, and cupping her cheeks, I inspect every inch of her.

"What happened?"

She tries to shake her head and even smiles at me, but the spark is missing from her eyes.

"Tell me what happened. I can't fix it if you don't," I insist.

"I just miss my dad. I spoke to him and got a little emotional. It's nothing."

I can't tell if she's telling the truth.

Her smile widens. "Nothing's wrong, Falcon." She takes hold of my hand and pulling it away from her face, she links our fingers. "I'm sorry for letting you wait on the roof. You still want to go up there?"

I nod because we will be alone, and it will give me a chance to find out if she's hiding anything from me.

***

My eyes are glued to Layla's face as she laughs at something Lake said.

I haven't heard anything from my parents since the fallout yesterday, and Layla reassured me she was just feeling sad because she misses her dad.

My phone beeps, and taking it from my jacket, I see a message from Julian.

The Rose Acre. Penthouse Suite. Meet me now.

"Guys," I say, shoving my phone back in my pocket, "I've been summoned. It shouldn't take long." Getting up, I place my hand on Layla's shoulder and lean down to press a kiss to her forehead.

"Is everything okay?" she asks, a frown of worry already forming.

"Yes, I'm just meeting Julian quickly," I put her at ease.

"Let us know if you need backup," Mason says, his eyes sharp on me.

"Will do."

I walk to the parking area and getting in my car, I leave the Academy. It only takes me a couple of minutes to drive to The Rose Acre. Giving the valet my keys, I walk inside the exclusive hotel, wondering why Julian wants to meet here of all places.

When I get to the suite, I knock, and a couple of seconds later, my bother opens the door.

"Come in," he grumbles, his eyes on the document in his hands.

Taking a breath, I step inside the room and shut the door behind me.

"Sit," he orders while taking a seat himself.

"I'll stand."

Julian drops the documents on the coffee table and glares at me. "Sit, Falcon."

"I'm not one of your employees you can order around," I remind him. "Why are we meeting here?"

Julian leans back against the sofa and rests his arm on the back of it. "Funny you should ask that. After the bomb you dropped, our family home turned into a battlefield."

Yeah, I can only imagine.

"I called you here because I have a question for you." He picks up the tumbler with whiskey from the side table and takes a sip.

"Ask."

"You're not marrying Serena Weinstock?"

That's the last question I expected from him.

Scowling, I walk to the other sofa and sit down. "No, I'm not."

"Are you serious about this girl," he pauses and gestures toward a newspaper lying next to him of the sofa, "Layla Shepard?"

My eyes focus on his, and I try to figure out where this is heading.

"I am."

Slowly, he nods then takes another sip of his drink.

"I'm willing to make you a deal," he finally gets to the point. "I'll marry Serena."

Shock vibrates through me, and for a moment, I can only stare at my brother. "Why would you do that?"

"Unlike you, I am prepared to conclude the business deal between our family and the Weinstocks."

"I'd congratulate you, but you'll know I'm not sincere. Before committing to Serena, I feel you should know she's unstable." I might not get along with Julian, but I don't want my brother marrying a potentially insane person.

"Oh?" His eyes show interest for the first time. "That might make things easier for me," he muses.

"In what way?"

"I can marry her then have her committed. That way, it's a win-win."

"Damn," I shake my head, letting out a burst of cynical laughter, "that's cold, even for you."

Julian tilts his head and jeers, "Aren't you lucky to have me for a brother?"

"That all depends on what your gracious sacrifice will cost me." I lean back, already knowing what he wants.

The corner of Julian's mouth lifts. "You know what I want."

I clear my throat and grin back at him. "Why would I give you my shares, Julian? I wasn't going to marry Serena in the first place."

"There are two contracts on the table." He gestures to them. "The first is where I buy your ten percent." When I open my mouth to tell him it will never happen, he holds up a hand. "The other contract is where you sign a promise that you'll never compete for the chairmanship, and you relinquish all rights to the Woodrow Wilson banknote. Sign either one, and not only will I marry Serena, but I'll back your relationship with this Layla girl."

My eyes sharpen on his, and it makes him smile triumphantly.

I keep staring at Julian, and maybe it's because of the time I spent with Layla, but instead of feeling bitter, sadness creeps into my heart.

What would Layla do right now?

"She'd look for the reason behind your behavior," I murmur, confusing the hell out of Julian.

"What?" he asks.

I sit forward and rest my elbows on my thighs.

Letting out a burst of silent laughter, I smile down at my hands as I link them.

"You're acting strange," he says as he sets down his glass. "Did you drink before coming over?"

I shake my head and reply, "I've just learned to look at things from a different point of view."

"What does that mean?"

Layla would be brutally honest.

Bringing my eyes back to his, I ask the only thing I've ever wanted to know, "Julian, why do you hate me so much?"

His mouth lifts in a smirk. "I don't hate you, Falcon. You're just competition."

Getting up, I walk to the windows and look out over the night lights.

"I never wanted any of this," I murmur. I close my eyes as years of bitterness and heartache comes to the surface. "I never wanted to be your competition."

"Bull," he laughs.

'Instead of me being your weakness, let me be your strength.'

Remembering Layla's words make my eyes burn. I close them, and as I turn around to face Julian, I don't hide my feelings.

There's no mask.

Just me.

The disappointment. The longing. The hurt.

Julian looks at me, and the smirk fades from his face.

"I never wanted to work in the company," I say, my voice low and hoarse. "I have different plans for my future, and it doesn't include CRC."

Julian rises to his feet, his eyes never leaving mine.

"What are your plans?"

A burst of air explodes over my lips, and I struggle to hold back the tears.

"None of you have ever asked me that question." Through the emotion, I smile. "I want to start my own business."

"You do? What kind of business?" Interest flickers over Julian's face.

Always the businessman.

"Buying patent rights." I take a deep breath, then share one of my dreams with my brother, "I want to help create the future. I want to help bring dreams to life."

"Really? That's actually a good idea. Do you have any prospected investors in mind?"

"Not yet. Why? Are you interested?" I let out a chuckle when he smiles.

"I'll invest anything you want if it means I get CRC."

I close my eyes as the blow hits.

Always CRC.

Opening my eyes, I walk to the coffee table and pick up the contracts. I shouldn't feel upset when I read through both, but it hurts more than I thought it would.

I look up from the papers and lock eyes with Julian. "All I wanted was a big brother. Just once I wanted to hear you tell me, I meant more to you than shares." Taking a pen from my pocket, I crouch down by the coffee table and begin to initial the pages of the contract where I renounce my rights to both the chairmanship and the banknote. When I get to the last page, I pause.

"Can you lie to me?"

"About," he whispers, which makes me look up at him.

When I see the emotion on Julian's face, I have to force the words out, "Can you tell me you love me and that you're proud of me?"

He clenches his jaw and glances to the windows.

He can't even lie to me.

I try to suppress the sob and quickly scribble my signature on the dotted line, then get up and leave the suite.

I jog down the hallway and slam the button for the elevator as I struggle to hold back the tears. Tipping my head, I watch the numbers blur, and the first tear falls as the doors slide open. I step inside, and when I press the button for the ground floor, I see Julian come out of the suite.

"Falcon, wait!"

I watch him run towards me as the doors begin to slide closed, not stopping them.

I'm so tired, Julian.

I can't fight you anymore.

The doors close right before Julian reaches the elevator.

"Goodbye, Julian," I whisper.

Instead of the elevator starting its descent, the doors slide open again, and Julian rushes inside. His body slams into mine and his arms wrap around me.

His breaths are coming fast as he tightens his grip on me. "I'm sorry." I close my eyes and press my mouth to his shoulder as a cry rips through me. "I'm so sorry," he whispers again.

I stand in my brother's arms and cry for everything I've lost, everything I never had, and everything I will never have.

"I love you, Falcon."

My heart aches from hearing the words. It's a physical pain, but healing at the same time.

I wrap my arms around him and grab hold of his jacket.

"I'm so proud of you, Falcon."

When the doors begin to close again, Julian stops it. With an arm around my shoulders, he pulls me out of the elevator.

We walk back to the suite, and after he shuts the door behind us, he asks, "Why did you sign the contract?"

Using my palms, I wipe my face. "CRC can't be a part of my life if I want to keep Layla."

"Do you care so much about her?"

I nod, and meeting his eyes, I say the words out loud for the first time, "I love her. I love every single thing about her. She's..." I smile because there's only one word to describe her. "She's color."

"If she means that much to you, I'll support you."

"Do you really mean that?"

His mouth curves into a warm smile, the same one he used to have when we were kids. "I really mean it."

He walks over to the side table and pours two tumblers of whiskey. "Have a drink with me."

Stepping closer, I take the glass from him, and he holds his up, toasting, "To surviving the curse of being a Reyes."

"That's one way of putting it," I agree.

"Let's sit." He walks over to the sofa, and as I take the seat across from him, he asks, "So how much do you need to start the business? Have you drawn up plans?"

I let out a burst of laughter.

Always the businessman.

Chapter 21

Layla

Worried about Falcon, I go sit outside our building on the pavement and stare up the road. For the hundredth time, I think about calling him, but not wanting to interrupt something important, I hold myself back.

Lights come up the road and hoping it's Falcon, I get up. My hope fizzles away when a black Rolls Royce pulls up in front of the dorm.

I step back to the entrance, and watch as the driver gets out and walking around the car, he opens the back door.

When he looks at me and gestures inside the car, I frown.

"Mr. Reyes would like a word with you."

"Me?" I point to my chest as shock ripples through me.

How did he even know I was sitting out here?

Are they watching us now?

Cautiously I step closer and peek into the car.

Mr. Reyes is busy reading a newspaper, as he says, "Spare me a minute, Miss Shepard."

"Yes, Sir," I say, and slide into the back.

The driver closes the door, and I feel a twinge of panic.

He won't hurt me. Right?

Folding the newspaper, he turns his head to me. "Let me have a look at you."

I sit frozen, not sure what I should do.

Meeting his eyes, my lips twitch when I see where Falcon got his intimidating look from. Falcon takes after his father.

"You don't look like Stephanie," he comments.

"I take after my father, Sir."

He nods, then states, "You and my son have caused quite the stir."

I keep quiet, just like I did with Mrs. Reyes.

"Leave my son, and I'll transfer an amount of your choice to your bank account."

I tilt my head, and not breaking eye contact, I stare at Mr. Reyes. There's no malicious expression on his face, not like with Mrs. Reyes.

He's testing me.

"No, thank you, Sir. I don't need money."

"That's a first. Is there a single soul on this planet who doesn't need money?"

"There is," A smile stretches over my face. "My dad."

"He's a traveler, right?"

I nod.

"How does he manage to travel without money?"

"You're right." His eyes sharpen on me. "Let me rephrase myself. I don't need your money. I have two wonderful parents who provide for all my needs."

The corner of his mouth twitches, and it helps ease the knot in my stomach.

"What are your plans for the future?"

Thinking carefully, I answer, "I'm going to travel with my dad."

"Sentimental but not very ambitious," he comments.

A soft smile forms around my lips. "Have you heard the saying; Beauty is in the eye of the beholder?"

"Yes." He turns more in his seat, showing interest.

"I believe the same principle applies to ambition. What you consider ambitious will not be the same for me." When he nods, I continue, "You've spent your life creating this…" I gesture to outside, "and it's nothing short of an empire. It brought you happiness to see it grow."

"Right," he agrees.

"My happiness lies in experiences. I want to stand in the place God created in anger, and experience the vastness of it. I want to stand where the Berlin wall once stood, and experience how much the world has changed."

Mr. Reyes features soften slightly, and I take it as a good sign.

"I care for Falcon. In the past few weeks, I've learned a lot about him. I truly believe we have a great deal in common. I would appreciate your approval, but it's not vital to the success of my and Falcon's relationship."

"I respect your opinions and outlook on life, Miss Shepard," he says while reaching for the newspaper. Opening it, he asks, "I'm right to say you will not be accepting any funds from me?"

"Yes, Sir."

"And you will not give up on dating my son?"

"Yes, Sir?"

"Then it's settled. I don't see any reason the two of you cannot date."

"Yes… wait? What?" My eyes widen in surprise, and I'm not sure I heard him right.

"You may date my son, Miss Shepard," he repeats, then glancing at me, the corner of his mouth lifts. "Like Stephanie said, you're both adults."

"Thank you, Mr. Reyes." I suppress the urge to hug him.

"Have a good evening, Miss Shepard."

"You too, Sir."

I open the door and get out. "Drive safely," I call before closing the door.

The driver nods at me, then gets back in the car. As they start to pull away, Falcon comes speeding down the road.

I pull a face and close one eye when it looks like he's not going to stop in time. My heart begins to pound with worry. "Shit, Falcon! Stop!"

When he hits the brakes, clouds of smoke come from the screeching tires.

The Rolls Royce stops, but I couldn't care less. I rush to where Falcon is getting out of the damn deathtrap, and bringing both my hands up, I shove at his chest. "What the hell? Have you lost your mind? Who drives like that? Give me the keys?" I hold my hand out to him, palm up.

Falcon places the keys in my hand, then looks over my shoulder. "What's my father doing here?"

"Don't try to change the subject!" I scold him. "You could've caused an accident."

"Falcon," I hear Mr. Reyes' voice behind me and turning around, I almost freaking curtsy.

This is really turning out to be a weird night.

"Sir," Falcon greets his father. "Why are you here?"

"I felt like a drive down memory lane." Mr. Reyes looks at the keys in my hand. "You'll be holding onto those, Miss Shepard?"

"Yes, Sir."

"Good. Make him suffer to get them back."

"I'll definitely do that." I shoot a glare at Falcon before walking to Mr. Reyes' side. "Let me walk you back to the car."

"You don't look like your mother, but you sound like her," he comments as we walk the short distance.

"I'll take that as a compliment," I tease.

"You better. Your mother is one hell of a woman."

Emotion totally overwhelms me and not thinking clearly, I throw my arms around Mr. Reyes neck and hug him.

"Thank you for being so good to my mom," I whisper.

He pats me twice on the back. "I should thank you for all the times I've stolen her from you."

Pulling back, I smile. "It's okay. I get to spend more time with Falcon, so I'm just stealing it back."

This time a smile forms around his mouth. "You do that."

He gets in the car, and I wave when they drive off.

"What just happened?" Falcon asks behind me.

Swinging around, I scowl at him. "You just lost your driving privileges, that's what happened."

"I'm serious, Layla."

"So am I." Pointing at my face, I ask, "Does it look like I'm joking?"

"No," he says, finally realizing I'm upset with him. "I'm sorry for speeding."

"And you won't do it again," I say.

"I won't do it again."

He tries to look apologetic and innocent, which draws a grin from me. "Not the same as Lake's. The hot, sexy look works better for you."

He smirks at me. "Oh yeah? Like this?"

I begin to walk toward my room. "Wait, tell me what happened with my father."

"We talked. We agreed. We hugged."

"You sound like my father now. It's scaring me," Falcon whispers.

I turn back around because the last thing I want to do is cause Falcon more worry, but then I see the mock look of fear on his face.

"Are you looking to get on my bad side, Falcon?" I ask, putting my hands on my hips.

"No," He closes the distance between us and leans down. "But, I am looking to get inside you."

"And here I thought you were a romantic," I mumble.

"I've now fucking seen it all," Mason says, sounding stunned.

"Right?" Lake asks.

Glancing over my shoulder, the two are sitting on the floor by the window.

"Why are you sitting there?" I ask.

"We saw the Rolls pull up, then figured we'd hang around," Lake answer.

Mason looks at Lake. "Have you ever seen Mr. Reyes hug someone?"

"He didn't exactly hug her back. It was more like an awkward pat."

"You're right," Mason agrees.

"Want me to confiscate your car keys as well?" I growl at them.

Mason is first on his feet and walking toward the exit. "Nope. I'm good."

Lake gets up and yawns as he stretches. "You love me too much to take my keys."

"Lake," Falcon snaps.

"Falcon," Lake grins, wagging his eyebrows.

We watch him jog after Mason, then Falcon wraps an arm around my middle and pulls me closer. There's a serious look on his face as he pushes me backward toward my door.

"Did my father say anything to upset you?"

I shake my head, and when I bump into the door, I reach behind me and open it. Once we're inside, Falcon kicks it closed.

"Did he really just talk to you?" he asks, wrapping his other arm around me as well.

I nod, then try to stand on my toes so I can kiss him, but he only tightens his hold on me so he can keep me in place while grinning down at me.

"Unfair," I complain.

"First promise me something," he says, the grin fading from his face.

"What?"

"You won't hide anything from me. If my parents do anything to upset you, please tell me."

"Okay." Falcon raises an eyebrow at me. "I promise I won't keep anything from you."

"Good." He loosens his grip, and I can finally stand on my toes. I press a quick kiss to his mouth then step out of his hold "That's it? Just a peck?"

"Oh, you have some promises to make yourself before you're getting any."

"A couple of minutes with my father, and you're already bribing me?" Falcon calls after me as I walk into my room.

I grab my pj's and walk to the bathroom, when Falcon comes in, and says, "Why are you going in there to get changed? I've already seen you naked."

I stop in the doorway and look down at the fabric in my hand as I admit, "That was in the heat of the moment. It will feel uncomfortable just dressing in front of you."

Falcon comes to me and taking hold of my chin, he tips my face up. There's a warm look in his eyes, and it makes me feel better. "That's okay. Don't ever do something you're not comfortable with."

"Thank you for understanding."

He leans down and presses a kiss to my mouth. "Is it okay if I stay over tonight so we can talk?"

I nod and slipping into the bathroom, I shut the door.

I quickly go through my nightly routine, and when I come out, Falcon isn't anywhere to be found.

Shrugging, I quickly go through everything I'll need for tomorrow's classes. I set my bag by the coffee table when the door to my suite opens. Falcon comes in, dressed in his sweats and a t-shirt.

"Are you ready for bed?" he asks, setting the keycard down on the table.

"Yes, it's been a weird day."

Once we're comfortable in our usual position, Falcon asks, "What did you talk about with my father?"

I glance up at him. "About ambition, experiences, The Skeleton Coast, and the Berlin wall."

Falcon tilts his head, a look of confusion crossing his features.

"We bonded," I explain in layman's terms.

"My father doesn't bond. With anything," Falcon states.

"Well, he did with me. I guess there's a first time for everything."

Falcon tightens his arms around me. "I've never seen my father hug anyone."

"Have you ever considered it's because no one hugged him?"

He thinks about what I said, then asks, "Honestly, I've never given it a thought."

"You might not like hearing it, but you're a lot like your father. You just need to find the chink in his armor."

"Which is?"

"Listening to what he has to say. Showing him that you understand him, even though you differ in opinion."

Falcon remains quiet, and I glance up again.

"Like you, Falcon. He wants to be seen."

Emotion washes over Falcon's face, and when I can see he's struggling, I sit up and pull him into my arms. I press his head to my chest and pulling my fingers through his hair, I whisper, "It's okay. You're all just a little lost. You'll find your way to each other."

Falcon nods, and wrapping his arms around my waist, he grips me tightly. Watching the emotional struggle play over his face makes tears flood my eyes.

After a while, I ask, "How did things go with your brother?"

Falcon doesn't answer me immediately, and I just continue to play with his hair.

"We talked and listened for the first time."

A small smile plays around my lips.

"First we fought, then we talked," he corrects himself. "Things aren't perfect between us, but it's a start."

"I'm glad to hear that." I take a breath, then say, "I met your mother yesterday."

Falcon sits up. "I knew something must've happened."

"Have you ever had dinner with your father and Julian? Just the three of you?"

"Why just the three of us?" he asks.

"After meeting your mother, I've been thinking a lot, and when I spoke to your father, it confirmed my thoughts for me."

"About my mother?"

"Yes." I take a breath, hoping I'm not making a mistake. "Your mother is a cold woman, Falcon. She might be responsible for a lot of the fights between you and Julian, and also with your father." When Falcon doesn't say anything, I quickly add, "I could be wrong. I don't know her so well. It's just, she reminds me so much of Serena."

Falcon lets out a sigh. "You have a point." He lies back again and pulls me to his chest. "I'll see if I can arrange dinner with my father and Julian."

"I think it will help you all."

He presses a kiss to my hair. "Thank you."

Silence falls between us, but after a while, Falcon whispers, "You sleeping?"

"No," I whisper back.

"Why not?"

"You haven't said it yet."

He lets out a chuckle. "Sleep my rainbow."

Chapter 22

Falcon

"It's okay, you can forgive Julian," Mason says. "I'll be the unforgiving asshole who'll remind him he was a bastard to you."

"I'm so glad I'm not going to work at CRC," Lake mumbles from where he's lying on the couch.

"You're awake?" I ask.

"Mhhh."

"At least we know he's alive," Mason grumbles. "How do you sleep so much?"

"Takes a lot of energy to eat," Lake mutters.

Mason laughs, "That's for fucking sure."

"Are you really okay with working at CRC?" I ask Mason.

He nods, then glances to where Lake is. "I'm more worried about him."

"There's nothing to worry about," Lake yawns and sits up.

"You sure? Marrying a complete stranger is totally okay with you?"

Lake begins to smile and taking out his phone, he looks at something. "I'm sure."

"What are you smiling at?" I ask, getting up from the chair on the balcony. When I get to Lake, he holds his phone out to me. I take it and look at the picture of a girl. A second later surprise ripples through me. "Is this her?"

"Who?" Mason almost falls off his chair in his hurry to get up. He comes and looks over my shoulder. "Hot, damn. Is this Lee-ann?"

"Yep." Lake lies back down with a huge smile on his face.

"The fucker has been playing us. Suffer my ass. He's getting the best deal out of the three of us," Mason complains.

I look down at the photo again. Her hair is a mixture of brown and red, and her eyes are dark. Her skin is so damn smooth she looks like a doll.

"She's beautiful," I say as I hand the phone back to Lake. "And you get along with her?"

"The times we've spoken have been okay."

"Lucky fucking bastard," Mason growls as he walks back to his chair. "You get a hot as hell girl, Falcon gets to start the new business, and me... I'm fucking stuck with Julian and our fathers."

Lake just chuckles as he covers his eyes with his arm.

Sitting down, I say, "Talking about fathers, I'm having dinner with mine tonight."

"You're shitting me."

"With Julian as well," I add.

Mason leans forward and looks at the sky. "Seriously thought it would start snowing now."

I kick the one leg of his chair.

"What made this miracle happen?" he asks.

"Layla."

"Yeah?" Mason actually looks impressed, which is no easy feat to achieve. "She's a miracle worker. Maybe I should ask her to do some of her magic on Kingsley?"

"Why?" I ask, stretching my legs out in front of me.

"She's acting weird. She used to give me shit until I made her my assistant. Now she's... just weird."

"You don't think it's because you almost drowned her?" Lake asks.

"It was the fucking shallow end!"

"Just saying," Lake mumbles.

We're having dinner in Julian's suite so we'll have privacy. Standing outside the room, I take a couple of deep breaths before I knock.

Julian opens the door and looks relieved when he sees it's me. "Thank God. I was worried Father would arrive first, and I'd be stuck with him."

I walk in, and we're just about to shut the door when we hear grumbling coming up the hallway, "Why do they always pick the top floors. All the damn exercise it takes to get to the room doesn't make any sense."

Father stops in front of the open door and looks from Julian to me. "Good, you're already here. Let's eat." He walks in and goes right for the table. Sitting down at the head, he glances around the room. "Don't you have any newspapers?"

I shut the door while Julian grabs the newspaper from the sofa. "Here you go, Sir."

Father takes it, and while opening it, he says, "Sit, the food's getting cold."

We take our seats, and Julian looks at me, then tips his head in Father's direction. I shake mine and raising an

272

eyebrow, I glance at Father just as he lowers the newspaper. We both school our faces at the speed of light, and you hear utensils clattering as we grab hold of them.

"How was the meeting with the…" Father frowns, then looks up at the ceiling, "who did you meet with again?"

"The Meesters. They're opening a new plant in Dallas," Julian reminds him. "It went well. We should be signing next week."

"Good. Good." Father turns his eyes to me. "Did you get your car keys back?"

"I did."

"Did she make you grovel?"

Before I can stop myself, a smile spreads over my face. "She did."

"Good. Good."

"Car keys?" Julian asks.

"Your brother was driving like a drunkard. Layla took his car keys. Quite like the girl's spirit."

"You've met her?" Julian asks Father.

"I did. We had a lovely talk." Father cuts a piece of his steak. After swallowing it, he asks, "Julian, aren't you interested in a woman?" Father glances up at the ceiling again, then forces the words out, "Or man."

When I see the flabbergasted look on Julian's face, I quickly duck my head and press my lips together to keep from making a sound.

Father picks up the newspaper and wacks me against the shoulder. "What? There's nothing wrong with it as long as your brother is happy."

"Oh God. Father, I'm straight," Julian exclaims.

I quickly cover my mouth, but it doesn't help as I burst out laughing.

"You are? Good, when can I expect my first grandchild?"

My laughter dries right up when Father looks from Julian to me.

I start shaking my head, which has Julian saying, "You're the one with the girlfriend."

"She's eighteen," I protest. "Besides, Layla would probably slap you upside the head for throwing her under the bus."

"I can see her doing that," Father agrees. "So, it's up to you, Julian. You are the eldest, after all."

Clearing his throat, Julian says, "I've been thinking about the business deal with the Weinstocks."

Father sets down his knife and fork, and his eyes snap to Julian. "Why?"

274

"They have leverage in the legal world."

"And?"

"What do you mean?" Julian asks, frowning.

"They better have more than a couple of contacts in the legal world if they want to marry their daughter off to one of my sons."

"You didn't agree to this?" I ask.

"Of course not! Have I ever said such a thing?" Father huffs. He gives Julian a hard look. "You will not marry that girl. Over my dead body. She's as loony as that mother of hers."

"I told you," I exclaim. "Didn't I tell you she's unstable?"

"Then why have you and Mother been putting pressure on Falcon?" Julian asks.

"Just your mother."

Julian leans forward. "If you didn't agree, why didn't you stop her?"

A slow smile begins to form around Father's lips, which has my mouth dropping open. "I was hoping all her nagging would help bring you and Falcon closer together." He shrugs. "And it did, so problem solved."

"Problem solved?" Julian growls. Shoving his chair back, he gets up. "And all the threats about the chairmanship?"

"Sit down, Julian. You're too old to be throwing a tantrum," Father scolds him. "Your grandfather taught me the best way to learn is through experience." Father stops and frowns. "Well, would you look at that. It's the same thing Layla said." He starts to nod, looking impressed. "Bright girl, but I digress." Father leans back in his chair. "It took longer than I thought it would, but you've come to an understanding, haven't you?"

I pull a confused face. "I'm not quite following."

"I threw a bone in a dog camp, expecting my sons to realize they weren't dogs, but wolves. Dogs fight over bones. Wolves hunt in a pack. They catch the big prey."

'Listening to what he has to say. Showing him that you understand him, even though you differ in opinion.'

"You wanted to make sure we would stand by each other during an attack," I say, finally understanding.

"Yes!" Father slams his hands down on the table. "Yes, my boy!" His face pulls with emotion as he rises to his feet. "How could I leave you my life's work if I wasn't sure you'd protect it." His chin starts to tremble, and it has me swallowing hard on the emotion. "It's not about the money.

You can always make more. CRC is our legacy. It belonged to my father and his best friends. It belonged to my best friends and myself. It will belong to the two of you, Mason and Lake. It's a legacy of trust, of loyalty…" Overwhelmed with emotion, Father slumps back down in his chair and covers his eyes with a trembling hand.

I look to Julian, when he says, "It's a legacy of brotherhood."

Father looks exhausted as he reaches into his breast pocket. He pulls out a box and sets it down on the table between Julian and me.

"Woodrow Wilson." He keeps his hand on the box. "Who will take over from me?"

I take a moment to gather my emotions. Standing up, I straighten my jacket and clear my throat, and then I hold my hand out to Julian. "I trust you and Mason will take good care of CRC."

Julian rises to his feet and placing his hand in mine, we shake.

When we take our seats again, Father slides the box to Julian's side. "Good. Good. You start tomorrow. I'll officially retire at the Thanksgiving celebration. You'll be inaugurated at a special board meeting, which will be held the Wednesday after Thanksgiving."

"So soon?" Julian asks, looking a little pale.

"I'm tired, Julian. She's a big ship to steer. I'm afraid if I continue to stay at the helm, I'll steer her into stormy seas."

I didn't even join the company, and I'm tired, so I can only imagine what my father must feel like.

"What are you going to do once you retire?" Julian asks.

"I'm going to have lunch with Layla and find out where that place is that God made while he was angry. That sounded interesting."

"You really like her," Julian affirms.

"I do. I do." An expression of loss crosses Father's features. "I suppose that's what happens when you grow old. You come face to face with your what could have been. You look into her eyes, and you see old dreams."

Holy shit.

Did he love Stephanie?

Chapter 23

Layla

This time I've borrowed one of Kingsley's dresses. I really don't see the need to buy a dress for the couple of occasions I'll attend in the future. We're both wearing tweed woolen dresses because it's cold, and we don't plan on freezing our butts off.

Once we're ready and it's time to go, we meet the guys in the lobby so we can attend the Thanksgiving function for CRC Holdings.

Falcon's eyes do a slow sweep over me, and then his sexy smirk comes out to play. "You look beautiful," he says, and the pride in his voice makes me feel really pretty.

"Let's get going," Mason says.

As we step outside the building, Serena walks towards us. "Who am I riding with?"

"You're going to the Thanksgiving function?" Falcon asks, not looking happy.

"Yes, your mother was sweet and invited me," she boasts.

"Luckily, my car only has two seats." Falcon walks to his Lamborgini and opens the passenger door, "Layla?"

I smile at him as I get in and hear Mason grumble, "Kingsley, you're with me. I'm less likely to kill you."

"I guess that leaves you, Lake," Serena says.

When we're all ready, Falcon pulls away, with Mason and Lake following. Looking out the window, I notice students stop and stare as we pass them by, and I slide down in the seat, bringing my hand up to cover my face.

Falcon lets out a chuckle. "Why are you hiding?"

Driving out of the gates of Trinity Academy, Falcon begins to speed up. "I'm not used to people staring, and you better not go over the speed limit."

"Yes, ma'am."

We enter a double lane, and Mason pulls up next to us. Glancing into the car, I see Kingsley staring out of her window, her head turned away from Mason.

"I wonder if they'll ever get along," I murmur.

"Who?" Falcon asks, not taking his eyes off the road ahead.

"Kingsley and Mason."

"I'm sure they will, eventually."

"I hope so."

We pull up to a hotel where the function is being held and getting out of the car, we all gather in front of the entrance before we go in.

"I have something to take care of," Serena says, and I let out a sigh of relief as she walks away from us.

"Thanks for that, guys," Lake mutters sarcastically.

"Always a pleasure," Mason teases.

When we walk into the designated hall, nerves begin to spin a web in my stomach until I see Mom. I wave at her, and when she comes over, I don't care about keeping up appearances and hug her.

"I missed you," I whisper, relishing in the feel of my mom's arms around me.

"I missed you, too." She pulls back and inspects my face. "You're doing okay, right?"

I nod. "Yes, I'm winning at this college thing."

Mom turns her smile to Falcon, "It's good seeing you again."

"You too, Stephanie."

Mom looks back to me, then mentions, "I spoke with your dad. He was a little worried about you."

I wave a hand, brushing it off as nothing. "I just missed him. I can't wait for him to visit."

"Only a couple of more weeks," she reassures me.

"Ahh… look who finally decided to join us," Mr. Reyes says as he comes up behind Mom. "Stephanie, I must compliment you on doing such a wonderful job of raising Layla. She's quite the woman."

"Thank you, Warren."

"Good seeing you again, Sir," I greet him.

"Father," Falcon says with a nod.

"You two enjoy the festivity." Mr. Reyes takes hold of Mom's elbow and guides her toward more guests who just arrived.

Soft piano music plays in the background complimenting the hum of voices as people stand and talk in small groups.

I lean closer to Falcon and ask, "What are we supposed to do?"

"Eat, smile, and then we leave after the announcement."

"What announcement?" I ask.

Falcon smiles and gestures to someone. Placing a hand on my lower back, he says, "Let me introduce you."

"You actually came," An attractive man says as he shakes hands with Falcon.

I immediately see the similarities. They're the same height and have the same dark hair with sharp features.

"You must be Layla," he says, holding out his hand to me. "I'm Julian Reyes, Falcon's brother."

Bringing a warm smile to my face, I take his hand. "It's a pleasure finally meeting you."

"Finally?" He raises an eyebrow and the corner of his mouth twitches. "Does that mean Falcon has been talking about me?"

The Reyes men all have the same gestures.

"I've only heard good things," I assure him.

"That's hard to believe," Julian teases.

"Are you ready?" Falcon asks him.

"As ready as I'll ever be." Julian takes a deep breath then looks around the room. "It's a little of an anti-climax now that the day is here."

"How so?"

Holding up a glass with amber fluid, he explains, "It feels like that moment you get your first car. There will never be a moment like it again. I'm sure I'll hate being the chairman six months from now."

Falcon lets out a chuckle. "Rather, you than me."

Someone catches Julian's attention. "It's time." He smiles at me. "It was nice meeting you. I'm sure we'll see each other in the near future."

I nod and watch as Julian walks to the front of the hall, where a small podium stands. Mr. Reyes is already behind the glass structure. He looks at Falcon and indicates for him to come up front.

"It will only take a minute. Get something to drink while you wait," Falcon says, and adjusting his jacket, he walks to the front.

Kingsley comes to stand next to me and hands me a flute. "Don't get your hopes up. It's not alcoholic."

I take it from her. "Damn, so much for hoping, but thank you, my friend."

"What was it like meeting Julian?" she asks.

I shrug as I take a sip of the drink, but the second it hits my taste buds, I cover the glass and spit it back out. I rush to the restroom and quickly rinse my mouth.

That was really stupid of me. I should've known anything bubbly in a flute would be apple juice.

"Are you okay?" Kingsley asks.

I pat my mouth dry, then answer, "Yes, it was apple juice. I'm allergic to strawberries, and apples are from the same family, so I just avoid it."

"Shit, I didn't know. Can you have grapes? There's chardonnay with a grape flavor being served, as well. I can get you one of them."

"Grapes are safe," I smile.

We go back to the hall, and as we walk in, Mr. Reyes says, "Thirty-two years."

Everyone grows quiet and turns to face the front.

Mr. Reyes places his hands on either side of the podium, his head bowed. Julian is standing to his right

Falcon, Mason, and Lake stand behind them, joined by Mr. Cutler and a man I can only assume is Mr. Chargill.

"Thirty-two years," Mr. Reyes repeats, then he slowly turns his head.

I lean closer to Kingsley and ask, "Is that Mr. Chargill standing next to Mr. Cutler."

Kingsley nods, then whispers, "Yes."

"Todd, do you remember how drunk we got after we signed our first deal?"

"You and Asher were the ones who got drunk. I, of course, was the designated driver," Mr. Cutler calls out.

"Oh, right," Mr. Reyes chuckles.

"I'll never forget the first deal we signed. It wasn't anything big, but the pride we felt." Mr. Reyes looks up and sighs loudly. "Lord, the pride we felt. It was priceless."

He bows his head again, and a couple of seconds pass. "The time has come for me to step down as chairman." Lifting his eyes to the audience, I begin to feel emotional when he says, "I'm so indescribably proud to announce that I will be handing over the helm to Julian, my eldest. I trust you will all show him the same loyalty which you've shown me."

Mr. Reyes turns to Julian and places his left hand on his shoulder while holding out his right. As Julian takes his hand, Mr. Reyes says, "Mr. Chairman, I hand CRC Holdings, and its legacy over to you with a peaceful and assured heart."

Julian slightly bows his head. "Thank you," he pauses for a second, "Father. I will do my best to fill the insurmountable space you will leave."

A round of applause sounds up, and I grin wide as I join in.

"I'll leave you to it then," Mr. Reyes says as he steps away from the podium to go stand next to Falcon.

Julian's eyes scan over the people who have all helped shape CRC into what it is today. "I've only been with the company for four years, and there were days I marveled at how my father, Mr. Chargill, and Mr. Cutler managed to handle it for thirty-two years." He smiles. "Luckily, I'll have all of you, and Stephanie has agreed to stay on as my assistant." Julian looks to Mom. "Thank you, Stephanie."

Mom nods at him, a proud smile on her face.

Julian turns, and I'm not sure who he's looking at, then he says, "Mason, will you join me."

Mason glances at his father, who nods for him to go.

"In six months, Mason will be joining us, and after a year, he will be inaugurated as the President."

When Mason is standing next to Julian, I wonder what it means for the future of the company that Falcon and Lake won't be joining them.

"I count myself lucky to know I'll have Mason by my side. I'm sure I can speak for both of us when I say, we have great plans for the future."

Mason's mouth lifts at the corner, and his eyes show no emotion, as he says, "Definitely."

"There goes the future of CRC," Kingsley grumbles softly next to me.

Mason gestures to Falcon and Lake, then adds, "Let's not forget Falcon and Lake. Even though they're only shareholders, they will play a big part in our future growth."

I smile as I look at the future of CRC. "I think they're all going to make a great team," I whisper to Kingsley.

Falcon

I'm standing with Mason and Lake, watching as the guests enjoy the selection of appetizers and cocktails.

"I think she'd give Lake a run for his money when it comes to eating," Mason suddenly says.

"Who?" Lake asks while trying to suppress a yawn.

"Kingsley." Mason gestures toward the banquet tables along the left side of the hall. "That's her third plate she's busy loading."

I smile when my eyes land on Layla, and she waves at me.

"Falcon," Mother says as she comes toward me, looking elegant as always. "Aren't you going to greet your mother?"

Keeping up with pretenses, I lean down and brush my lips over her cheek. "Mother."

"Doesn't Serena look beautiful tonight?" she asks, smiling toward the table where Serena is helping the servers arrange the food.

"I haven't noticed."

A scowl quickly settles on Mother's face.

"Why is she here, anyway?" Mason asks, much to my surprise.

"I invited her, of course."

Mason ignores the disapproving look on my mother's face, then states, "She better enjoy it. Once I take over, that will change."

"Honestly, Mason. Your aggression toward Serena is uncalled for," Mother snaps.

Mason lets out a dry chuckle. "Uncalled for my ass."

Mother focusses her dark scowl on him. "It astounds me how Asher and Candice managed to raise such an imprudent son."

"Mother," Julian says as he joins us, "stirring the pot as usual?"

Gasping, she turns to Julian with wide eyes. "I'm doing no such thing. The boy doesn't know the first thing about being respectful."

Julian smiles politely, and taking hold of Mother's elbow, he whispers, "Respect is earned. Leave them be and go talk with the other wives."

Her eyes dart sharply over us before she gives in and does as she's told.

"Wow, she listened. Shows you the power of a title," Mason mutters.

I glance over the food area, and not seeing Layla, I keep scanning through the room. My eyes fall on her, where she's standing with Stephanie and Kingsley.

She drops the plate she was holding, and when Stephanie takes hold of her shoulder, I begin to walk toward them.

Suddenly Layla sinks to her knees, and panic flashes over Stephanie's face. Alarmed, I begin to run, and when I reach them, Layla coughs as if something is stuck in her throat.

"She's choking?" I ask, moving in behind Layla, who scares the shit out of me when she slumps backward, losing consciousness.

"No, it's an allergic reaction," Stephanie says, an urgency to her voice while she digs in her handbag. She pulls something out, which looks similar to a marker. "Hold still, kiddo. Mom's got you." She places her left hand on Layla's thigh then jabs the pen hard against the outer side of Layla's leg. "Five, four, three, two, one," she counts before removing it. Glancing up at me, she asks, "Has anyone called 911?"

"I don't know." I shift my body so I can slide my arms under Layla, and picking her up, I say, "I'll get her to the hospital faster."

As I turn and begin to run toward the exit, Stephanie calls after me, "Tell them I administered an EpiPen!" The last thing I hear from the hall is Stephanie yelling, "Lake, get your car!"

Mason darts by me, and I hear him shouting at the valet, "Cars! Now!"

There's a rush, and as soon as my car pulls up, Mason opens the passenger door. I set Layla down on the seat and strapping her in, my eyes dart to her face. It looks like she's been in a fucking fight and lost. Fearing the worst, I run around the car.

"I'll clear the way for you," Mason says as he slams the door shut and rushes toward his Bugatti.

Mason quickly starts his car and shoots past me. As I pull away, I glance in the rearview mirror and see Lake and Stephanie getting into his Koenigsegg Regera.

I don't care about speed limits as I press my foot down on the gas, and luckily, the first light is green. We weave our way between the other cars, and nearing a light which just turned yellow, Mason floors it. The Bugatti rockets forward, and as the light turns red, he brings the car to a screeching halt in the middle of the intersection, the ass of the car swerving to the side.

I fly past him, and he takes off, repeating the action at every light until we finally reach the hospital. Speeding toward the side where the emergency entrance is, I slam the brakes too late and turning the steering wheel sharply, I bring the car to a jolting stop as the left backside hits a pillar.

I rush out of the car and quickly get Layla.

"Allergic reaction. Her mother gave her an EpiPen," I ramble the information to the first emergency staff member I see.

It feels like I'm caught in a nightmarish daze as I set Layla down on the bed they point out to me. My steps feel unbalanced as I slowly move backward.

I look at all the people rushing toward her, but I can't hear what they're saying as they begin to work on Layla.

Someone places a hand on my shoulder, and through the haze, I see Mason.

When Lake comes to stand on my other side, covering his mouth with both his hands as if he's praying, the thought hits.

What if I lose Layla?

Chapter 24

Falcon

We're still standing to the side when I hear a nurse talking with Stephanie.

"Her blood pressure has come down from one-forty-two over eighty-nine, to one-thirty-three over ninety-three. She's responding to treatment. We're going to move her up to ICU so we can keep an eye on her."

Stephanie nods. "I'll go complete the paperwork while you get her settled." She even smiles at the nurse before she walks over to us.

How is she so fucking calm?

My world is lying unconscious on a hospital bed, looking like she's been beaten to within an inch of her life.

Stephanie gives me a comforting smile, which isn't comforting at all, seeing as I can see the worry in her eyes. "She will be fine, Falcon. Don't worry. She had the EpiPen, and the doctors are taking care of her."

"Will –" My voice is too hoarse, and I clear my throat. "Will she be okay?"

Stephanie looks at the three of us, then points to a waiting area. "Layla will be fine after all the effects wear off. It's happened before, and as long as we act quickly, she's fine. Honestly, the three of you look worse. Go sit down. I'll get you all something to drink after I've signed all the forms at reception."

We do as we're told, and when we're sitting, Lake asks, "Are those normal numbers for blood pressure?"

"Fuck if I know," Mason whispers, as he places his hand on my shoulder again as he leans back, crossing a leg over the other.

We're all fucking whispering, still scared out of our minds.

I glance at Mason's hand, then say, "I'm not going anywhere."

"It's not because of you," he mumbles. "It's for me. So I don't do anything stupid right now."

"What are you talking about?" I ask.

"Just crazy talk. Don't mind me."

I sit back and really look at Mason. When I see the lethal gleam in his eyes, which is usually only reserved for West, I ask, "Who do you want to kill?"

"Serena," he spits the name out. "She served the dishes. Before tonight, I've never seen her lift a fucking finger at any of the functions we've attended with her. She handed Layla that plate. She's a TA. She has access to student records. My gut tells me she found out about the allergy."

"Come on," Lake jumps in. "I don't like her either, but that's pushing it a bit."

"My gut has never been wrong," Mason murmurs.

That's true.

I replay the night from the moment we got to the hall. Serena leaving us to take care of something. My mother not once saying anything about Layla.

"Are you sure you saw her hand Layla the plate?" I ask to make sure.

Mason nods while clenching his teeth. "It caught my eye because I thought it was weird that Serena was smiling at Layla."

"My mind's a bit slow. Can you remember if my mother said anything about Layla?"

All three of us think about it.

"I don't think so," Lake answers.

"Are you thinking the same thing as me?" Mason asks.

"I'm too scared to answer that question. I don't know what I'll do if we're right."

Mason stands up. "You won't have to do anything. I'll handle it." He leaves the room without telling us where he's going.

I turn my head to Lake. "Go with him."

"You sure?"

"Yeah, Stephanie is here, and I'm sure Kingsley will be here soon."

When Lake runs after Mason, and I'm left alone, my suspicion begins to grow until an uncontrollable anger's burning in my chest.

God help them if they had anything to do with Layla being in the fucking ICU right now.

Layla

Waking up, it feels like my head's about to explode.

It takes me a moment to remember what happened, and I'm not surprised when I hear the beeping of machines. Someone's holding my hand and opening my eyes, I turn my head to the right where I see Falcon sitting next to the bed. He lifts his head and presses a kiss to my fingers before he closes his eyes.

"I'm okay," I whisper.

His head snaps up, and when he sees I'm awake, he darts out of the chair. Sitting down on the side of the bed, he rests his arms on either side of my head and leans in close. The worry etched on his face makes him look older than twenty-two.

"How do you feel?" he asks while his eyes drift over every inch of my face.

"I'm sure I look worse than I feel," I joke. "Not pretty right now, right?"

His eyes lock on mine, and the loving smile on his face makes emotion push up my throat. "You're beautiful."

When my face crumbles and the tears rush to my swollen eyes, I turn my head away from him.

Falcon pushes his arms under me and holds me tightly. He presses a kiss to the side of my temple, and I turn my head further away, really not wanting him to see me looking like this.

I feel him brush my hair back, and he presses another kiss to my jaw. "You'll always be beautiful to me." Kiss. "Thank you for waking up."

"I don't want you seeing me like this," I admit tearfully.

Falcon takes hold of my chin and pulls my face away from his arm. "Look at me." When I don't, he repeats, "Look at me, my rainbow." I bring my eyes to his, and he smiles again. "I love you."

Hearing the words while I look my worst has my heart overflowing with love for this man.

Leaning down, he kisses my swollen lips. "I love you, Layla."

Falcon keeps brushing his hand over my hair while looking at me until Mom comes to stand on the left side of the bed.

"How do you feel, kiddo?"

"Better," I answer. Confused, I ask her, "What did I eat? I had a sip of apple juice, but I spat it out immediately and rinsed my mouth. I can't believe I had such a bad reaction to it."

"You're allergic to apples, as well?" Falcon asks as he moves back to the chair on my right.

"They're part of the same fruit family," Mom explains. "There's a whole list of fruits she has to avoid." Mom smiles, reassuringly at me. "I'll ask the doctor."

Falcon gets up, taking his phone from his pocket. "I need to make a quick call. I'll be right back." He walks out of the room, and all I hear is, "Mason. Layla had apple juice."

Falcon

"She did?" Mason asks.

"Yeah, they just told me there's a whole list of fruit Layla can't have."

"So it's not Serena's doing?" he asks, still not sounding convinced.

"No, for once, she's innocent."

"I'm watching the security footage for the function, and it shows Serena carrying only one pie, and it's the one she gave to Layla."

"Drop it, Mason," I say, feeling exhausted. "Layla said it herself, she had apple juice." I take a deep breath. "Let it go. You're looking for something that's not there."

"Okay."

"Is Lake with you?" I ask, wanting to make sure Mason doesn't do anything stupid.

"Yes, he's hovering over my shoulder as we speak. Take the phone." I hear them pass the phone, then Lake says, "Hey, is Layla better?"

"She is. She's just swollen from the reaction. Don't come by yet. It will only make her feel uncomfortable."

"Okay, but keep me up to date."

"I will. Thanks for everything tonight. Tell Mason I say thanks."

"I will. Try to relax."

We cut the call, and when I walk back into the room, Kingsley is with Layla.

"I'm so sorry. I wish I had known," Kingsley says, looking like she's been crying all night.

"It's okay, really. I should've known better," Layla argues.

"I could've killed my best friend," Kingsley sobs.

Layla gives me a pleading look, on the verge of crying again. I put an arm around Kingsley. "Hey, these things happen. It's no one's fault. The important thing is Layla's okay."

Kingsley shakes her head and crying harder, she buries her face against my chest. I hug her, keeping my eyes on Layla.

"Thank you," she whispers.

I nod, then pat Kingsley's back.

Chapter 25

Layla

After recovering, I've been spending a lot of time with Kingsley. We've been planning the ski trip, and we're busy going over everything while doing facials.

"I've made the payment for the cabin," I confirm. "The guy said we can get there any time after three pm."

"Great." Kingsley lets out an evil-sounding cackle, then says in a sing-song voice, "The guys are going to shit themselves."

I laugh at her. "Come on, the place isn't that bad."

"For them, it's a couple of levels lower than hell," she explains.

"I don't want them to hate the trip," I muse, "Maybe I should look for a better place."

"No." Kingsley leans over the coffee table and grabs my phone from my hands. "You would be happy staying there, right?"

"Yes, but that's me."

"Isn't the whole purpose of you getting to plan the ski trip, so the guys can experience a different kind of vacation?"

"It is," I admit. I hold my hand out. "Give me the phone, I won't change a thing."

Kingsley gives me a stern look, "Promise?"

"I promise."

When I get my phone back, I double-check that the payment went through for the Ford Transit, and when I confirm it, I tick it off the list. "The van's booked as well. Now, all we need is to get snacks for the ride."

Kingsley laughs again. "No private jet. Tick. No five-star resort. Tick. No gourmet chefs. Tick."

"You're making me feel bad," I grumble at her, dropping my phone on the table.

"Sorry, I'm just enjoying this so much."

I pick up a candy bar and point it at her. "You do realize you're going with. Sitting in the back with Mason and Lake. Tick. Sharing a room with Mason and Lake. Tick."

She finally realizes, and a painful look crosses her face. "Oh shit." She falls back on the couch. "And just like that, you popped my bubble."

Falcon

"Dafuuuc?" Mason asks as we all stand outside the dorm, staring at the huge-ass van, Layla rented.

Lake places his arm around Mason's shoulders, "That, my friend, is our ride to hell."

Mason glares at me, then grumbles, "The fucking things I do for you."

Glancing at Layla to make sure she's not offended, I see her and Kingsley doing their best to not laugh, and epically failing at it.

While everyone loads their baggage into the back, I place my arm around Layla and leaning in, I whisper, "You're enjoying this, aren't you?"

She nods, grinning wide. "It's going to be so much fun."

"I'm willing to bet my left nutsack it will be anything but fun," Mason mutters as he opens the side door. "These seats better unfold into five-star fucking beds."

He climbs inside, and Lake follows him with an unsure look on his face.

When Kingsley gets in, Mason says, "Don't come back here, Hunt. Traveling in this thing is torture enough for me."

"Wasn't planning on coming anywhere near you, Asshole," Kingsley bites back.

"Children, Daddy's had a long year, and he'd like to relax. Try to get along because we're stuck in this thing for the next seventeen hours and Layla's driving," Lake says, his voice overly patient as he reclines his seat and closes his eyes.

I get in the front passenger seat, and Layla climbs in behind the steering wheel.

"Layla's driving?" Mason grabs hold of the headrests in front of him. "Hold up. I'm getting out."

Layla starts the engine and pulling away, the van jerks a couple of times before she presses down on the gas, making it shoot forward.

I quickly put on my safety belt and glance over my shoulder when Mason complains, "I'm going to fucking die."

"Would you shut up already?" Kingsley snaps.

"Don't you tell me to shut up, Hunt. I'll throw you out of a moving van."

Kingsley's reply is to shove her right arm into the air, giving him the middle finger.

"Is that the same finger you use to masturbate?"

"What the fuck, Mason?" I shout from the front.

"I'm going to throw *you* out of a moving van," Lake threatens and getting up, he climbs over to the seat so he can sit next to Mason. Glaring at him, Lake snaps, "I dare you to say another word."

"It's okay, guys," Kingsley says. "It's not like I'd expect any better of him."

I look at Kingsley to make sure she's okay. "You want to sit up front with Layla?"

"I'm really okay," she whispers to me.

"We can switch when we stop for a restroom break," Layla says, quickly glancing at Kingsley in the rearview mirror.

Kingsley smiles. "It's cool, guys. Let's enjoy the trip."

Layla

I park the van and switch off the engine. Getting out, I stretch, feeling stiff from the four-hour drive.

I walk around the van, and when Mason gets out, I grab hold of his arm and pull him to the side.

"What?" He snaps at me.

"Don't ever talk to my friend that way again and don't spoil this week for everyone." I take a deep breath and encourage Mason to do the same. "Come on, take a deep breath. Chill. Let's have fun."

He just keeps glaring at me.

"Why are you so upset, Mason? No one forced you to come."

"Cool. I'll just grab a cab and go back home," he sneers. When he takes a step to the right to walk around me, I move with him. "Layla," he warns, his voice dropping low.

I lock eyes with him, and we stare at each other for a couple of seconds. Mason's mouth sets in a grimace, making him look pretty scary.

I reach up on my toes and throw my arms around his neck, hugging him tightly.

"What the fuck are you doing," he growls.

"I'm giving you a hug. I care about you. I want you to have fun with us. I don't want you being angry all week," I ramble.

A couple of seconds pass, and then I feel his hand press against my back, instead of pushing me away.

"Take a deep breath," I whisper.

He listens and does it a couple of times.

"Do you feel better?" I ask.

"Yeah," he answers, sounding much calmer.

I pull back and smile up at him. "Want to eat anything? I'll pay."

He glances at the convenience store. "Is it safe to eat anything from there?"

I let out a chuckle, and taking hold of his hand, I pull him toward the entrance. "I'm sure we can find something."

While I'm paying for the coffee and donuts, Falcon comes to stand next to me.

"I saw you talking with Mason. Is everything okay?"

I nod and give the cashier the cash. "Yeah, he just needed to unwind."

"Thanks for that. Not many people have patience with him."

Falcon picks up the coffee holder, and I grab the bag of donuts. "I'm just mentioning this, so you know and not to cause trouble. Kingsley is scared of Mason. Can you talk with him, just have him ease up on her a bit without letting him know what Kingsley said?"

"She is?" He asks. "She told you this?"

"Yeah. She says it's because he's so aggressive," I explain.

"Are you okay with Mason?" he asks.

I nod. "Oh, yeah. I know he's a good guy underneath it all."

"Good. I'd hate it if you didn't get along with him or Lake."

"They're good people." I grin up to Falcon so he won't worry.

"Come, kids," Lake calls out. "I'm driving."

"You sure?" Falcon asks.

"Yep." Lake climbs in behind the steering wheel and leans over the passenger side as he calls out to Kingsley. "Sit up front with me."

We all get in, and while waiting for Mason, I hand out the coffees.

"Oh look, here comes my eldest," Lake says, which has me chuckling before I grab a donut from the bag.

Falcon

"We survived the drive," I say, setting down my bag in the middle of the living room. I glance around, then up at the ceiling, and when I see all the cobwebs, I mumble, "That might change, though."

"Did you find this place after watching a horror movie?" Lake asks.

"It's not that bad," Layla says. "Let's get settled in, then we can go see what the rest of the students are up to."

"We get to go to the resort?" Lake asks, a hopeful look lighting up his face.

"Of course. We're on a ski trip with them." Layla says, a worried look settling on her face. "If this is too much for y'all, then don't force it. We can stay at the resort."

"We're just fucking with you," Mason says, throwing his arm around her shoulders. "So, this is what they call roughing it?"

"Nope, that would be a tent in the middle of the woods," Layla replies. "This is… ahh… a level beneath roughing it."

Mason looks at Layla and chuckles, "In other words, this is roughing it level four." He nods and letting go of her, he walks to the sliding door. He tries to open it and has to yank at it a couple of times, which has Lake laughing.

When Mason finally has the door open, he turns around, and throwing his arms in the air, yells, "Level up!"

After deciding who sleeps where we unpack some of our things.

Seeing Kingsley head down the stairs, I jog to catch up with her. "Hey, Kingsley. Can we talk?" I ask, pointing toward the sliding door.

"Sure." She follows me outside and asks, "What's up?"

Taking hold of her arm, I make sure Mason doesn't see us and pull her out of the view of the living room.

"Layla mentioned you feel uncomfortable with Mason," I explain. "I just wanted to reassure you that he's really harmless. He'd never hurt you."

Kingsley glances out over the nature around us and wets her lips before she says, "I don't want to make a big scene about it. I'm learning how to handle him."

"Will you tell me if he ever crosses the line?"

"Won't it be too late then?" she asks.

"True. Let me rephrase that. If he acts in a way that really scares you, tell me so I can deal with it before it gets out of hand."

She nods, and a slight smile forms around her mouth. "Thanks, Falcon. I'm probably overreacting. I mean he's friends with you and Lake, so I'm sure I just have to get to know him better."

"He would never physically hurt you," I reaffirm.

"Deep down, I know that," she admits. "I'll try and be more patient with him."

"Thanks, Kingsley." I gesture to the door. "Let's go see if the others are ready to head to the resort."

Chapter 26

Falcon

After having some hot chocolate at the resort and getting the schedule for when we can go up on the mountain, we return to the cabin for an early night after all the driving.

Yawning, I stretch out on the bed while waiting for Layla to finish in the shower.

When she comes into the room and turns off the light, I move over to the left side and wait for her to lie down before I wrap an arm around her so I can pull her closer.

Laying face to face, she asks, "How was your first day at Camp Layla?"

Chuckling, I answer, "I'm not going to lie, it was quite the experience." It's definitely not what I'm accustomed to, but I can't say I hated it.

"Good or bad?"

"Surprisingly good." Wanting to be close to her, I whisper, "But I'm hoping it's not over yet."

"Yeah?" She moves her right hand to my chest and brushes it down to my abs. "Your abs are my absolute favorite part of your body," she murmurs.

I lift myself up on my left arm and push her onto her back before I lean down and press my mouth to hers. I had full intentions of going slow until my tongue slips inside her mouth. It feels like forever has passed since our first time together.

Brushing my tongue against hers, I mimic what I want to do to her. Licking and biting, I forcefully kiss her until she moans into my mouth. I reach for her shirt and breaking the kiss, I breathlessly say, "I want to feel your skin against mine."

Layla nods quickly, which has me removing her clothes as fast as I can. The urgency to be with her is making me lose my damn mind.

"I want to thrust into you until you're screaming my name in ecstasy," I whisper hoarsely as I cup her breast, squeezing hard while my mouth crashes down on hers.

I want to come inside you.

I want to fuck you so badly I can't think straight.

Sliding my hand down, I slip it between her legs, and when I push a finger inside her and feel how wet she is, I don't even think to remove my sweats. I just shove the fabric down, and freeing my cock, I position it at her entrance. I thrust in hard, and it feels so fucking good, I have to rest my forehead on the pillow next to her to take a moment to regain control over my body.

Layla's arms wrap around me, and using her nails, she drags them down to my ass.

Fuck.

It takes a lot of effort to not just slam into her until I find my release. I lift my head and locking eyes, I warn her, "If you do that again, I won't be able to go slow."

"Promise?" she teases, and bringing her hands back up to my shoulders, she drags them down slower and harder than before, driving me wild with desire for her.

Bracing myself on my right arm, I drive into her with every bit of strength I have. Layla tilts her head back, her lips parting on a moan. Lowering my head, I latch onto her neck, and I suck as hard as I'm fucking her, wanting… needing to leave my mark.

This woman.

She's the only one who has the power to make me lose total control.

Needing to feel all of her, I press my chest to her breasts and moving both my hands down the side of her body, I push them under her and grab hold of her ass. I bury my face in her neck, and my hips move faster, hitting the sweet spot within her. Creating a perfect rhythm, my body shudders from how good it feels.

Layla presses her mouth to my shoulder, muffling her moans as her body begins to convulse under mine. The sound, along with the feel of her orgasming, makes me tighten my hold on her ass so I can move faster.

"Oh, God... Falcon," she cries, her body arching into mine.

Breathless and high on ecstasy, I groan, "Fuck."

I'm addicted to her. To the feel of her wetness coating my cock while her inner walls grip me tightly.

I pound into her, and when the moans of her ecstasy fill my ears, pleasure sizzles down my spine, and my body begins to shudder as I empty myself in her. I keep moving, needing to spill every drop inside of her.

The satisfaction is so intense, spasms of pleasure keep rippling through me, making me slowly rock into her until I let out a breathless groan as my body stills.

After the pleasure fades away, I can't bring myself to move off of her. I turn my face to hers and press kisses along her jaw while she catches her breath.

"Making love to you is like having an out of body experience," I whisper by her ear.

"Definitely," she agrees, sliding her hands up my back. "Can we sleep like this?"

Layla

Joining Kingsley in the kitchen for coffee, I try to be as casual as possible when I ask her, "Did you sleep well."

"I was out cold," she says. "I thought I'd have to do fifty position changes and a sacrifice to the gods to fall asleep in the strange bed, but the second my head hit the pillow, it was lights out for me."

"Oh yeah," Mason says as he walks into the kitchen. "What would you sacrifice?"

Kingsley's eyes flick to him. "You really want me to answer that?"

"Coffee can wait," Lake says as he turns around in the doorway and heads back out.

I let out a burst of laughter and call after him, "I'll make you some and bring it to the living room."

Mason opens one of the cabinets, and a critter scattering out of it's hiding place, scares the hell out of him.

When he screams, hitting a high note I didn't even think was possible for him, I crack up laughing.

"Fu-uck. Fu-uck. Fu-uck. What the fuck was that?" He freaks out while recoiling away from the cabinet.

Kingsley bursts out laughing, instantly sinking to the floor as she points at Mason.

"There's a sacrifice for you, Hunt." Mason tries to regain his composure, but when he glances at the open cabinet, I almost wet myself.

"Fucking sharing the cabin from hell with the wildlife," he mumbles as he stalks out of the kitchen.

When Kingsley and I finally manage to stop laughing, I go back to preparing the coffee, including a cup for Falcon as well.

Arms come around me, and Falcon rests his chin on my shoulder. "Are one of those for me?"

"Yes." I turn my face to him, a happy smile playing around my lips.

He gives me a quick kiss, then whispers, "Why don't we stay here while the others go ski? I can think of a couple of things we can do."

"As much as I like that idea, I don't think they'll let us stay behind."

"True." He reaches for a mug and presses a kiss to my cheek. "Thanks for the coffee."

After we've all had coffee, I say, "It looks like everyone's awake." I glance at Lake, who's stretched out on the couch. "Well... almost all of us. Lake, are you sleeping?"

"I'm awake," he mumbles.

"Let's get going then." Clapping my hands together with excitement, I mention, "I've never been skiing, so today should be interesting."

"Don't worry, I've only been once, and all I can remember was the cold," Kingsley says.

"Mason's pretty good," Falcon mentions. "And Lake... ahh..."

When Falcon pauses, Lake lifts his head. "Hey, at least I don't fall down anymore."

"True, you just need to learn how to stop," Mason jokes with him.

"Can you ski?" I ask Falcon.

"I'm not the best, but I can manage," he replies, and wrapping an arm around me, he pulls me closer.

"He's lying, Layla," Mason mentions. "He taught me how to ski."

"You did? Will you teach me? Then I don't have to get an instructor."

A scowl darkens his face. "Instructor? What instructor? If you let some guy anywhere near you, there will be a murder up on that slope."

I let out a burst of laughter and wag my eyebrows. "I saw this cute instr –"

My words are cut off when Falcon ducks down, and picking me up, he throws me over his shoulder. A smack lands on my butt, making me laugh.

He stalks out the front door, grumbling, "Cute my fucking ass."

Between laughing and trying to breathe while hanging upside down, I get out, "She… is…. really…. cute."

Falcon stops by the van and sets me back down on my feet. "She?"

I nod, my eyes watering. He takes hold of my chin and presses a hard kiss to my mouth. "I'll teach my woman how to ski."

My woman. Sigh.

We meet up with some of the students from the Academy while we're waiting for our turn to go up on the slope.

"My ears are freezing. They feel like two blocks of ice," Kingsley complains, pressing her headband down on her ears.

Mason steps in behind her and moves her hands away. "What are you doing?" Kingsley scowls, but before she can turn her head toward him, he places his hands over her ears, and leaning forward, he blows hot air between his cupped hand and her ear.

Lake, Falcon, and I can only stare in shock while Kingsley freezes as if someone just poured a bucket of ice over her. She begins to blink faster, her voice sounding cautious as she asks, "Ahh... what's happening right now?"

"I'm being nice," Mason mutters before warming her other ear.

Kingsley's eyes dart to mine where I'm still staring at them, not quite processing what I'm seeing.

Mason adjusts the headband, pats her on the back, and walks toward the ski lifts that are coming in.

"Should I worry?" Kingsley asks, her eyes darting between Falcon and Lake. "Do you think maybe he's lost his mind?"

Lake rubs a hand over his jaw, then says, "I'm actually not sure."

"See, when I'm nice, you all think I'm insane. Get your asses to the lifts, so I can push Hunt down the slope." Mason gets on, growling under his breath, "Can't fucking win."

"He's fine," Falcon says, nudging my back to get me walking.

The view as we go up with the ski lifts is incredibly beautiful. When we reach the top, Falcon helps me to get all the gear on. He takes hold of my hands and pulls me into a standing position.

"Bring your legs together before you do the splits," he chuckles.

Hopping, I close the gap, then grin up at him. "Do I get to ski now?"

He lets out a bark of laughter. "No, you get to stand and watch me."

The moment he lets go of my hands, I tumble backward, landing on my butt. "It's okay, I'll sit and watch you," I laugh while shaking the snow from my gloves.

"I'm going to do a couple of short runs, so you can see the motions and what I do to stop. After that, you'll try a short distance."

He makes it look so damn easy as he pushes away and effortlessly makes a zig-zag pattern.

"Oh shit. Oh shit. Oh shit," I hear Kingsley panicking, and glance to my right. She's about to lose her balance when Mason comes up behind her and putting his hands on her hips, he helps her regain her balance.

Skiing away from her, he shouts, "Try not to break your neck, Hunt."

She somehow makes it to me and then falls back. "It's much harder than it looks."

"Yeah," I agree. "At least we're not the only ones who suck." I point to a group of students also trying to stand without falling.

"Layla," I hear Falcon say, and glance up at him. "Are the two of you going to just sit and chill, because I can head down then?"

"Oops, I forgot to look." I make a cute face and hold my hands out to him. "I'm sorry."

He shakes his head and grinning he takes hold of me and pulls me up. "I'm going to ski backward. All you have to do is follow."

We spent the morning having fun. I almost fall, but Falcon catches me, and as I smile up into his eyes, I can't believe how happy I am.

Holding onto him, I glance over my shoulder, and my eyes skip from Lake to Kingsley to Mason.

How freaking lucky am I to have this amazing group of people in my life?

ASPEN, Colorado – Two people were caught in a skier-triggered avalanche off the west side of Aspen Mountain this morning.

The disaster was triggered by a skier, who after skiing about 50 yards down the slope, caused a large avalanche to break. The slide caught the two skiers below him, according to the Pitkin County Sheriff's Office. They were part of a group of students.

One of the skiers was swept about 100 yards down the slope, and buried, but escaped with little injury, the sheriff's office reported. There's an ongoing search for the other skier who has been missing for over two hours. Authorities are using 'cell phone triangulation' to pinpoint the skier's location.

To be continued in _Mason_'s book.

Trinity Academy

FALCON

Novel #1

Falcon Reyes & Layla Shepard

MASON

Novel #2

Mason Chargill & Kingsley Hunt

LAKE

Novel #3

Lake Cutler & Lee-ann Park

Enemies To Lovers

Heartless

Novel #1

Carter Hayes & Della Truman

Reckless

Novel #2

Logan West & Mia Daniels

Careless

Novel #3

Jaxson West & Leigh Baxter

Ruthless

Novel #4

Marcus Reed & Willow Brooks

Shameless

Novel #5

Rhett Daniels & Evie Cole

Connect with me

Newsletter

FaceBook

Amazon

GoodReads

BookBub

Instagram

Twitter

Website

About the author

Michelle Heard is a Bestselling Romance Author who loves creating stories her readers can get lost in. She loves an alpha hero who is not afraid to fight for his woman.

Want to be up to date with what's happening in Michelle's world? Sign up to receive the latest news on her alpha hero releases → NEWSLETTER

If you enjoyed this book or any book, please consider leaving a review. It's appreciated by authors.

Acknowledgments

Sheldon, you're my rainbow. Thank you for all the color you add to my life.

To my beta readers, Kelly, Kristine, Elaine, Sarah, and Sherrie - Thank you for being the godparents of my paper-baby.

Sheena, Allyson, and Leeann - Thank you for listening to me ramble, for reading and rereading every book, and for helping me to create. I'd be lost without you.

Candi Kane PR - Girl, thank you for being patient with me and my bad habit of missing deadlines.

Wander & Andrew – Thank you for giving Falcon the perfect look.

A special thank you to every blogger and reader who took the time to take part in the cover reveal and release day.

Love ya all tons ;)

Made in United States
Troutdale, OR
11/18/2024

24991736R00184